Samuel's Pride Series Book 1

By

KATHI S. BARTON

World Castle Publishing, LLC

This is a work of fiction. Names, characters, places, and incidents are products of the author's imagination or are used fictitiously and are not to be construed as real. Any resemblance to actual events, locations, organizations, or person, living or dead, is entirely coincidental.

WCP

World Castle Publishing, LLC
Pensacola, Florida

Copyright © Kathi S. Barton 2013
ISBN: 9781629890166
First Edition World Castle Publishing, LLC October 15, 2013
http://www.worldcastlepublishing.com

Cover: Karen Fuller
Photos: Dreamstime & Shutterstock
Editor: Eric Johnston

Chapter 1

Samuel leaned heavily against his car as the big earthmovers smoothed out the ground once again. They'd been working hard since he'd gotten there over thirty minutes ago, and he was about to leave when a cruiser pulled up behind him and the officer got out.

"Sheriff." The man nodded back to him and leaned against his car with him. Neither man said anything, but Samuel didn't really care. He'd figured that sooner or later the new owners would call someone to have him run off. But he had one more thing to do before he left this area, and no one was going to stop him. He wasn't his father, and the sooner these people figured it out, the better.

"He's a bit nervous. Says he's afraid that you'll change your mind or some shit." Samuel nodded, still not saying anything as Sheriff Ross continued. "I don't know what the hell you'd change your mind about, but there you have it. Some people are just plain stupid if you'd ask me."

"He doesn't have a thing to worry about. I'm done with this area as of the moment we signed off on it." Samuel glanced at Ross when his radio squawked. "Tell him I'm just making sure, that's all."

Ross walked away, but Samuel could still hear him. He had a keen sense of hearing, so it was no problem for him to hear the sheriff telling someone that he was there now and nothing much was going on. Smiling, Samuel thought the man sounded as irritated as he was about the whole thing. When his mom touched his mind, he welcomed her like a warm blanket.

Is it gone? He told her it was. *Good. Nobody will have to feel the nightmares we went through while we were imprisoned there. You make sure that it's destroyed for me, for us, son.*

He can't hurt us anymore, Mom. I swear to you. He'll never be able to hurt either of us again. She sniffled, and he felt the pang in his heart that had been there for many years with no sign of relief until York Enterprises had made him an offer on the place that he couldn't refuse. He had only his father to deal with now, and Samuel wasn't worried about him in the least.

See that he doesn't. I'll kill the fucker if he touches you now. Samuel might have thought that funny if he didn't believe her. *I'm not taking his crap any more. The state of Illinois can have him now.*

The house and the ninety acres around it had become his the moment his father had defaulted on the loan. Then there were the unpaid taxes that Samuel had paid off, too. The city had been more than happy to have his name on the paperwork, and then fifteen days later he'd sold to York. The city was still trying to find his father for a great many other debts he'd incurred before skipping town over three months ago.

When will you be coming home? I've been getting used to this house, and I think I can live here. He had to laugh. His mother had fallen in love with the big house the moment he'd shown it to her. *The staff you have here is really nice, too. I like Butler. He makes me laugh.*

He's a good man. And when the rest of them get there tomorrow, you'll have to sort them all out again. I won't be able to get there until next weekend. I have a buyer for my condo coming in, and then I have to pack up my office. He stood up when Ross came back to where he was standing. *I have to go, Mom, you know how to get in touch with me if you need me.*

I do. I love you, Samuel. You be safe and keep an eye out for him. When he finds out what you've done, he's not going to be happy. Samuel hoped his father wasn't the least bit happy; in fact, he was looking forward to it.

Getting into his car after telling Ross he was leaving, he drove to his condo. There were boxes of his crap everywhere, and if truth be told, most of them had been sitting in the same place since he'd moved in over five years ago. Samuel didn't spend a great deal of time at home when there was work to be done.

Going to his bedroom, he pulled off his tie and tossed it to the chair. He wanted to think he could leave it there and not bother with it, but went to pick it up and hang it on the tie rack before he finished undressing. He had two meetings in the morning, and one of them was going to make him twice as rich as he was now.

His father, Sam Payne, had beaten the shit out of him for the last time on his seventeenth birthday, and Samuel had only gone back three times in all the years since; twice to visit his mom, and the last time to stay with her at the hospital when his dad had knocked her down a flight of stairs. She was hurt so badly that she was now confined to a wheelchair for the rest of her life. His dad had hurt her for the last time that day; Samuel was going to make sure of it.

Samuel had come up from nothing about ten years ago when he'd decided that he'd had enough of working for others and branched out on his own. Now he had more money than he could spend in two lifetimes and would soon have a great deal more. Life was suddenly going right for him and his mom.

By ten o'clock, after going over all his notes twice more and making sure the contract was perfect, Samuel went to bed. He closed his eyes, smiling about how happy he was going to be to start again, this time with the much-needed capital he'd had to scrape for before. He was asleep in ten minutes. Rarely dreaming, this time was no different than before. He wasn't a sound sleeper, but he did rest well.

He was up forty minutes before his alarm sounded, and out the door well before his offices opened. Today was going to be a great day. Samuel contacted Lilly, his secretary, from the back of his limo on the way in.

"Have coffee and other things sent up to the conference room. I don't think the little shit will eat any of it if he shows, but someone there might want to fortify themselves with something. Oh, and make sure that the liquor cabinet is locked and nothing is out where he can get into it." Lilly laughed as he continued. "I really hate this little fuck."

"Yeah, me too. But I like his dad. He's a good man." She asked him a couple more things, and then told him that Shriver and his lawyer were on their way in. Their estimated time of arrival was forty minutes.

"And this will ensure that you're going to have all the employees working even after you take over." The little man, August Shriver, sat at the table across from him. Samuel wanted to punch him in the face just on principle. He nodded at the contract and signed his name to his with flourish. Once again, Samuel glanced at Shriver's attorney, who did nothing but play on his computer. Neither man read the contracts being signed once.

"You should know that I'm only buying this from you because my daddy said I had to find gainful employment or he'd cut me off without a dime." He laughed. "I guess he wasn't aware that my employment was going to cost him so much."

Samuel had a feeling this was going to end badly. He almost felt sorry for the elder Mr. Shriver but let it go. You reaped what you sowed, and it seemed that this man had done nothing to curb his son when it came to ethics. As soon as the last signature was put on the right line, Samuel put all of his copies in the file and watched in horror as the other lawyer shoved them into his briefcase without any thought to where they ended up. As soon as the check was in his hand, Samuel stood up.

"You're staying around to help me make the transition, right?" Shriver seemed to be more interested in his nails than Samuel's answer, so when he didn't say anything, the man finally looked at him.

"I already did that. The last two weeks were for you. I cleared my calendar for you, and you never showed." Samuel moved to the door as he finished speaking. "I'm afraid other than cleaning out my office, my time here is finished. You should have shown up when you said you would."

"I was busy. Did you know that if you go to another country and you have your own plane you still need a passport? I didn't. But I do now." The man grinned, and Samuel opened the door. "You really aren't going to help me, are you? I'll just have to tell Dad to cancel payment on the check."

The lawyer leaned over to him and whispered in Shriver's ear. It was the first time the man had said a word the entire time. And now he was explaining to the idiot that had just given him a four million dollar bank check that there was no way to do that. They were still arguing over the check when Samuel walked out, closing the door behind him. He looked at Lilly Jacks and rolled his eyes.

"I gave my notice this morning." He nodded at her, thinking that it was a smarter move than he'd thought it was last week. "And Mr. Shriver senior is on line one. He said not to tell you if the son was around. He said it's important."

"Come inside so you can be a part of this. I'm not having this man take back the money. I've worked too hard now to give this up." He would, he supposed. The younger man was going to ruin this company and there wasn't a damned thing he could do about it other than back out of the sale. Samuel picked up the phone and pressed the speaker button. "Mr. Shriver, if you're thinking to have me not sell to your son, it's already over."

"Good. I was hoping you'd not back out. As much as I hate to say it, the boy is a fool. And an idiot." Lilly laughed and then changed it to a cough. Shriver senior didn't seem to mind the laughter. "He's going to fail, and we both know it. It's why when I lent him the money, the clause I had was when he didn't make it work after thirty days, I would step in and take it. It's my money, after all. The reason I'm calling is that I'm sending a man over to get some information from you. I know you're planning to stay in town for a few more days, and I'm going to take advantage of you if you'll let me. I think I'm going to need to have the information sooner rather than later."

"You do know that you're not teaching your son a damned thing by stepping in." Samuel didn't care if he pissed the man off or not. He was moving out now and didn't care really how many toes he'd stepped on. It was time to say what he thought and damn the consequences.

"Oh, but you misunderstood me. I'm not just taking over. When he fails, and he will, I'm going to cut him off without a cent. He was to find a job, make it work for one year, or I was done with him. I've set it all up with lawyers. August signed off on the contract this time, and there were enough witnesses that he'll never be able to come back on me again."

Samuel was wrong about the son and father it appeared. They were nothing alike. He smiled when he thought of the look on August's face when the shit hit the fan. And he was pretty sure August's father, Aggie, was going to enjoy it as well.

They made arrangements for him to send a man to come in that afternoon. No time like the present, he told Samuel. The man had even convinced Lilly to hang around for another month with the promise of a fat bonus if she did. Everyone was happy when they hung up. Samuel looked at Lilly as she sat before him.

"Do you think it'll work out the way he wants it to?" Samuel told her he didn't know but hoped so. "Me too. He seems like a nice man. I would hate to be in August's shoes when he finds out about all this. I mean, if it really comes to pass."

"I think it would be worth hanging around for." She nodded. "Will you try to get security to videotape it for me? It might make me laugh when I'm bored out of my mind one day."

She stood up laughing. "You'll never be bored. There is always some project you're going to work on, in the process of finishing up or one that you want to sink those teeth into. The only time I think I've ever seen you bored is when you took me to that gala thing last weekend. That was boring, by the way."

He worked with Tom Brinton for nearly five hours. The man took copious notes and seemed to ask a thousand questions. Samuel didn't mind. They were well thought out and things he might have asked if he needed to run this business. He handed the man some notes he'd made to give to August if he would have asked for them.

"These will be helpful. I don't know…. I had no idea that you were actually the businessman here. There are…I'm sorry, you must think I'm an idiot." Samuel shook his head and smiled. "I've only been working for Shriver Incorporated for about three months. Before that it was with a firm where everyone else did the work and the owners sat back and raked in the money. Mr. Shriver is the same as you about work ethic. His hands are right in the middle of things."

Brinton left after making arrangements to come in over the next few days. Neither of them expected August to show up to work, but that would just make things simpler for the rest of the staff. He was somewhat of a night owl, Brinton had said. Samuel was headed back to his condo when his phone rang.

"Cook has quit, sir. He said that he'd rather live on his retirement than move to the small town. I believe his wife is behind this move." Samuel shook his head. A house full of people and no one too cook for them. Butler, his butler, continued before he could tell him what he needed to do. Sometimes he forgot the man served in three wartime kitchens. "Your mother and I have put an advertisement in the paper. We've already had a call. Apparently they put those sorts of things on the Internet quickly. We have decided that if we get more than one applicant we shall have a cook off. Your mother thinks it would be fun."

"I'm sure she does. However you want to do it, Butler. I'm okay with it." He had a sudden thought. "Make sure whoever you hire can cook for a large staff, and if need be, when we entertain. I don't want some short order cook there thinking that he only has to cook for three people."

"I've already sorted that out, sir. I've put in the advertisement that one must be willing to be flexible, too. I should not think that having someone here that can do short orders would last long in this house either." Samuel agreed.

He'd told Butler that he was a were-lion. His mother was as well, of course, but she no longer shifted because of her back. Samuel hadn't wanted to find himself at the wrong end of a shotgun if anyone came across him in the yard. Peter Butler had only nodded and said that he'd known there was something special about him and was glad it wasn't nearly as bad as he'd thought it might be. When asked what he'd thought, Butler had declined to answer.

"Just keep me informed as to what you and Mom come up with. I'm going to be here until next weekend at the very latest. There are some things I want to finish up. Then I'll be done with this place." Butler said that he'd do just that. "And please be careful of my mom. She'll try her best to do much more than she should."

"Sire, if your mother wishes anything from us, and it is within my power to give it to her, she shall have it. And I believe you underestimate your mother's strength."

Samuel thought at times he did too, but she was his mom, and she would not be hurt ever again. Not so long as there was breath in his body.

~~~

"Okay, yes, I can be there. What do you need me to bring to your place?" Kennedy Buehler looked over the notes she'd taken since the woman had called her back about the job. She had to be there at nine in the morning to fix dinner for the staff, and then they'd have the interview afterwards. She assumed that she'd be cooking for the household, but a job was a job, and she'd take it.

"Oh no, we'll make sure you have what you need by the time dinner rolls around." There was a good deal of humor in the older woman's voice, and Kennedy felt herself smile in return. "I did mention that there might be some big entertaining, didn't I, dear?"

"Yes, ma'am, you did. Said there would be some bigger parties and that I would be feeding the staff. You mentioned, too, that they're not into vegetables much but can eat them." Strange thing to tell a cook, but it was their house. "I'll be arriving at nine, just as you said."

The woman made sure twice that Kennedy had the correct address, and for some reason, Kennedy thought that she'd not lived there long. First there was the fact that she'd had to ask the address of someone and she'd fuddled the house number twice before she'd said that it was right. Kennedy pulled her coat tighter around her as she walked back to her camper. Just four more months.

She was actually hoping things were to finalize sooner, but that wasn't something that she planned on. Only recently, when she'd come to Ohio to find a good job and make a living, had she realized all the hoops you had to work through if you didn't live in the state. Her family wasn't too happy with her at the moment either…especially her brother, but they'd get over it. She was twenty-six years old and needed to be out from under his rule.

Shamus was the head of the household. Not that she'd listened to her father overly much when he was in charge, but since Shamus had taken control of the family and all that went with it, Kennedy had been used and abused enough. Her father had been indulgent while Shamus hurt her. Thanks to her grandmother she'd been able to escape her home, where her family stayed most of the time, and come here. That had been just nine months ago. A great deal had happened in that little time.

She had hoped to get a house or, at the very start, an apartment. But her first attempt at either of them had failed. Kennedy had no bank account, and without an address, she wasn't getting one. And no one would rent her even a room without some sort of bank affiliation. Getting a job had proven difficult, too.

Her slight accent had made people think she wasn't a citizen, and she'd had to have her grandmother send her birth certificate. Kennedy had worked very hard at hiding her slight brogue, but there were times when it slipped up. After waiting for a week for her certificate, she'd applied at seventeen jobs and had been turned down flat. It wasn't until she came to this place that she'd been able to find a place to sleep and somewhere that would help her out.

Mr. and Mrs. Tucker and Amy Savage owned and operated Savage Park. It was a nice campground that catered mostly to pop-up campers and RVs, but a few tenters always came in. Kennedy had been able to pick up a tent really cheap; little did she know that it was cheap for a reason. The thing leaked like it was its job. After three weeks of moving from one spot to another trying to find a reasonably dry place, they'd asked her what was going on. She'd thought they were going to toss her out, but instead they had offered her one of the pop-ups in exchange for her helping around the grounds.

It wasn't what she'd been trained for, but it was a job that included room and board, as well as a little extra on the side. And when they'd closed down two weeks ago, she'd been asked to keep an eye on the place, as well as make sure that no one used the place without permission. She was going to watch the place through the winter, and by then she'd have established herself with an address and could get a bank account. Then an apartment.

The camper had a small heater, but there was a refrigerator and a stove. The camper itself was tiny, so the heater worked out well, she supposed, but winter hadn't hit yet, so she was hoping she'd be warm when the time came to use it in earnest. And she'd been able to have it parked next to the showers and bathrooms when they'd closed up, so that wasn't so bad either. Unless, of course, she had to get up in the middle of the night to pee. Then it was a cold and dark walk.

After fixing herself something quick for dinner, she went to the small laundry house to wash up her weekly clothes. There wasn't much with it just being her, but she wanted to start the week off tomorrow with fresh, clean clothes in the event that she got the job. The Savages said that if she ever found herself in a position to get something more, she was to take it, but she'd already decided that she'd do her damnedest to keep both jobs until they returned from Florida in a few months.

By ten she was in bed. She'd emailed her grandmother what was going on, then watched a movie on the old television that had been in the camper. The picture was crappy, but it was noise until she went to sleep. By ten-thirty she was curled up in her blankets and sleeping bag and asleep.

The dream always started in the same way. Her grandmother was there sitting in her usual place at the head of the table when she was home. Her mother and father were to either side of her, Shamus and her sister were seated next to their mother, and Kennedy to her dad's right. The butler brought in the first course of the meal and sat the large tray before her grandmother, who was speaking to her son.

"You should simply let me take her back with me. It will do me a world of good, and I'd very much love the company." Kennedy tried not to be too excited at the prospect of spending the summer with her grandmother. "You're not going to miss her, and you know it."

"She only just returned. I've a mind to keep her to meself for a week or two." Kennedy looked at her da and wanted to hug him to her. She knew he'd been teasing her and that it was as good as settled. "Mayhap we'll get you with your new man. He's been willing to wait on you all this time. I think it's about time you...."

When he stood up suddenly, she did as well. Her father was her world next to *seanmháthair*, and when he gripped his chest and looked at her, Kennedy could see the panic and pain in his eyes. Before anyone could move to help him, he fell over dead. Massive heart attack, they'd told them.

That had been nearly five years ago. Since that time she'd run to the States to hide from her brother. As it was, she'd been in and out of the hospital more times than she had her entire life before then. Shamus wanted her to heel, and she wanted to fly. But when he'd ordered her to marry a man nearly her own father's age, she'd told him no. He'd beaten her so badly the medics had been called, and she'd been carted off to emergency. Five weeks later, she was getting off the boat in the United States and had never looked back.

Chapter 2

"You should have seen it, Samuel. When the cover was lifted, there were five carrots, two pieces of red pepper, as well as a small onion. And there in the middle of this were three of the smallest pieces of beef you've ever seen." Samuel laughed at his mom's description of their first encounter with a cook, an Allice Anderson. It had not gone as well as they'd planned. "I had to have Butler go and ask her if this was a course or something. He returned to tell me that she said it was the main course and that dessert would be served when things were cleared. They were cleared as far as I was concerned. Why, I could have eaten it all in two bites."

"I'm assuming you didn't hire her." His mom sputtered and told him no. "Too bad. I was thinking I could stand to lose a few pounds."

"You'd lose a great deal more than that if you hired her. And you're not going to believe this, but she asked me what time I wanted her to come back tomorrow. As if she'd already gotten the job." She snorted at him. "I told her we had other applicants and that she would be notified. Had the nerve to tell me that she would be waiting, that by the end of this 'farce,' she called it, that we'd be begging her to come back. Over my dead body."

"Who do you have coming in tomorrow?" He'd called every night and had heard the update on the cook offs. The first person that had shown up had taken one look at the kitchen and declared it too beneath him to work there. The second wasn't much better in that he'd told them that he would need a staff all his own and that he didn't actually cook but had assistants do it for him. Today was the meal of the tiny meat.

"Kennedy Buehler is coming in tomorrow. Nice enough on the phone. She even asked me what she needed to bring with her." His mom yawned, and he deiced that he needed to try and get home sooner to help her. "I've had a really long day. I think I'll retire soon."

"I should get to bed too. They're coming to get the last of the things from the condo tomorrow, and then for the rest of the week, I'll be living in a hotel room. Expect the trucks to come sometime on Friday to drop off my things." She told him she would and yawned again. "I love you, Mom."

"And I love you as well. I'll see you in a few days, son." She laughed a little before continuing. "Butler has the local pizza place on speed dial in the event this Buehler doesn't work out."

Samuel spent the rest of the night working out the notes he wanted to go over for tomorrow. Aggie had shown up today and had as many questions as the man he'd sent over to learn what there was to know. In all the time since the papers were signed, over eight days ago, August hadn't been in once. The father was looking more and more like the newest owner.

The next morning started off as usual. Samuel answered emails that had come in and had set up a staff meeting so that Aggie, as he'd asked to be called, could meet them all at once. By the time the meeting was ready to take place,

Samuel had set up a couple of meetings for someone to work in the kitchen at his home and also make arrangements for a car. He hadn't had one in a good number of years, always relying on a limo service, and was excited to drive again. When Aggie showed up at ten after nine, Samuel knew something had gone wrong.

"August has a girl pregnant." Aggie said as he paced the office. "What the hell do you suppose he's thinking when he pulls his dick out? 'I'll just have Daddy take care of anything that goes wrong?'"

Samuel didn't answer the man, because frankly, he wasn't sure what to say to him. He'd already told the older man of the information that August had given him in the event the business failed, and this shouldn't have been a big surprise. Aggie continued pacing as he spoke.

"I've taken matters into my own hands and have had him removed from the house. As of now, he is no longer a son of mine. And security has been informed that if he comes to the building that they are to call the police and have him arrested for trespassing." A good start, but there was more he could do, but again Samuel kept his mouth shut. "I've also gotten with the attorneys and had them draw up the papers that give me this business. You're leaving it in good hands."

"I had my doubts, if you want to know the truth." Aggie nodded and sat down. "Shall we get to work then? I've a mind to get home. There are some issues that need my attention, and, frankly, I want to start a life of leisure."

Aggie snorted. "You'll never make it. I bet within a month you'll have another business going. If you don't meet yourself a girl first. There's a lot to be said to have the right woman."

"I've no desire to find even the wrong woman." Samuel pulled out some of the notes he'd been thinking to share with

Aggie and started work. By seven-thirty both men had made a great deal of headway, and Samuel was thinking that he'd be home Thursday instead of Friday now.

~~~

The house, if you thought of it only as a house, was easy enough to find. Kennedy arrived at ten minutes till nine and pulled her car into the space where the man on the intercom had told her to park. Gathering up her things, she moved toward the back door and was surprised when the door opened suddenly and a very staunch man stood there.

"Miss Buehler, I presume?" She nodded. "I have been informed by the missus of the house to show you around the kitchen and ask you for a list of supplies you might want for your meal."

"Aye," she said with a flush when he raised a brow at her, but she recovered quickly. "I was thinking to make chicken. How many do you think I'll be feeding?"

"Eight. The missus will join us, of course. We serve at six on the dot." She looked around the massive kitchen and let out a low whistle. "This is the main kitchen, and there is a larger one in the lower levels that will house the parties when they entertain. You'll be expected to be able to use both rooms."

He took her to the pantry that was only about half filled yet still held more items in it than she'd seen in well-stocked restaurants. There was also the storage room that she was able to live in if the need ever rose, as it was as big as three of the campers she was currently living in. She moved with him, taking out her notepad and writing down everything that she saw in the event she might need something. Then he took her to the dining room.

"The dining room will seat fifty, if need be. The lower levels will accommodate as many as five hundred if the doors are opened to the outdoors. The kitchen below us has an elevator in the event that both kitchens are needed. We have yet to use the lower levels, but the rooms are set up." Kennedy nodded, wondering if the people who lived here were famous. Not that she cared; she just wanted to be able to cook.

"And today? Will I be working alone or is there a staff in place? I can do an eight on my own, but I don't want to step on anyone's toes at the start." He looked at her oddly but only nodded at her.

"There will be a staff, and the person who is hired as the main cook will hire their own staff. You will be able to feed us today then without any issues?" She smiled at his question, wondering what they'd gone through in the past few days.

Kennedy knew that she wasn't the only applicant for the job. Two people she knew of had come already. One was Claris Todd. She was a bitch of the highest order but could and would run a kitchen with an iron fist. And she'd put out some really good meals. She just wasn't very nice. Then there was Allice Anderson. Allice was a nice enough person but temperamental and thought that what she cooked was the best. Even if it was a tad on the uppity side.

By the time they'd finished the tour of both kitchens, Kennedy had a better understanding of what she was applying for. It wasn't just a staff cook as she'd assumed, but someone as head of the kitchen as well as chef. She could and would be able to fill both jobs, thanks a great deal to her experience and education. When they entered the kitchen, there was an older lady sitting in a wheel chair that had to be the missus, and another woman who introduced herself as Brigitte Butler.

"I'm Summer Payne. You must be Kennedy Buehler." Kennedy took her hand and was surprised by the strength. "You'll be cooking chicken for us I understand."

"Yes, ma'am, if you want. I can do just about anything." The woman nodded and looked at Butler, as he'd asked her to call him. "I was wondering how you wanted it cooked. I can do anything from comfort food to five-star."

"I think after this week we've had I'd prefer comfort. I'll leave you to sort that out." She started to roll out of the room but stopped and looked at her. "Where are you from?"

It was on the tip of her tongue to tell her Ohio, but she knew that she'd heard her accent. "Ireland, ma'am, though I was born here. My parents moved here for a year before going home sometime after my first birthday. I was educated in France as well as the States." She nodded and left the room.

Around eleven-thirty, three younger women came into the kitchen. Kennedy had gone over the pantry and found that other than the chicken everything she needed was there. She was making a list for a menu when the other women started pulling bags of sliced meat from the refrigerator. Kennedy watched them for several minutes until they pulled down a large can of vegetable soup.

"You're not going to eat that, are you?" All three of them looked at her. "I can throw something together for you if you want. You don't have to eat that stuff."

"You can cook us something? It won't count." The bravest of the three little maids blushed. "We're the upstairs maids, and it's our turn to cook lunch until someone is hired."

"I won't tell if you won't." Kennedy pulled things from the refrigerator and started cutting and chopping. When she'd laid out her packet with her knives fastened securely in it across the large butcher block, the girls giggled. In forty-five minutes she had a nice light soup simmering, a salad made with the greens that had had to be cut up a lot to save even that much, and sandwiches…thick roast beef sandwiches with homemade honey mustard and Swiss cheese. The bread had been stuffed in the cabinet, but it was still not overly hard. By the time lunch was called, Kennedy was back to making her list.

"This is amazing." Mrs. Payne had joined them at the kitchen table, which surprised Kennedy. She didn't look up when one of the girls thanked her. She said she wouldn't tell, and she wouldn't. Besides, it had made her feel better about cooking in the big kitchen to break the ice, so to speak, with lunch.

"We had help. Ms. Buehler took what was left in the ice box and came up with this." Caroline, the girl who had spoken to her first, nodded in her direction. "She said she didn't feel right being here and not working."

"It was simple. They would have done the same thing." Kennedy walked to the pantry, embarrassed more than she could have said. When she returned, Mrs. Payne was sitting at the table with Butler and his wife. They asked her to have a seat. It came out more like a command, but Kennedy sat down.

"You're not going to get brownie points by sucking up." Kennedy stood up but sat again when Mrs. Payne told her to. "You'll learn that I'm mistress of this house, and when I tell you I'd like to have a conversation with you, you'll listen to me."

Kennedy took a deep breath and stood up. She wasn't going to be ordered around again, not even for a job. She moved back into the kitchen and started cutting up the three chickens that had arrived an hour ago. When she finished with them and had them soaking in buttermilk, she went back to the dining room to find that Butler and his wife were still there.

"I will cook for you tonight, as I've already started the meal, but I won't be treated like a child and ordered about like I'm a slave." Before she could turn and leave again, Brigitte asked her to please sit. "Am I being ordered to or asked?"

"Asked. I would wish that you'd have a seat." Kennedy sat down and waited. "The meal you're planning for this evening, will it be as good as lunch?"

"I should hope so." Then Kennedy flushed. "I don't care for canned soup, and the lettuce they were using was out of date and needed some trimming. That's all I did. The sandwiches were simply meat on bread."

"But it was more than simply meat on bread, and we both know it." Brigitte looked at her husband, then at her again. "You'll do well to listen to Mrs. Payne. She's a wonderful lady, but the past three cooks have been...let us just leave it at she needed to make sure you knew that she was in charge."

Kennedy nodded. "So long as she knows that I'm not a person who will tolerate being talked to like that. She wants something from me, then I can get it, but I won't let someone command me into anything again."

Mrs. Payne came in just as she was frying the chicken. Kennedy had planned on making chicken and dumplings but had found the corn meal and decided that she'd make cornbread, and that didn't go with dumplings. Mrs. Payne wheeled her chair to the opposite side of the counter where she was working and asked for a glass of water.

"I've brewed tea if you've a mind for it." She smiled and nodded at her. "There is sweet and not sweet. Which do you prefer?"

"Sweet please." After setting the iced glass of tea in front of her, Kennedy went back to work. "I'm sorry for the way I treated you. I should never have snapped at you."

"Mrs. Brigitte told me a little while ago that you had a row with the delivery man." She nodded at her. "I took care of him for you. He won't be giving you grief again."

"You did?" Kennedy nodded at her question. "I'm not a cripple. Well, I suppose I am, but there was no reason for him to speak to me like I…well, like I did you."

"When I'm nervous or afraid, my accent gets the better of me. The more I'm emotional the deeper and heavier it gets. And when that happens, people start to treat me differently. As if I'm a stupid woman who knows no better. I'm very intelligent and have a good education."

"People should learn to judge others by their works not what they see and hear." Kennedy put the last two pieces of chicken in the skillet as she checked on the cornbread. Dinner was in thirty minutes, and Caroline had come in to set the table for them to eat.

"May I ask you a question?" Kennedy nodded at Mrs. Payne. "Would you have taken credit for lunch had Caroline not told us what you'd done?"

"No. What would have been the point?" Caroline muttered *because it was good,* but Kennedy ignored her as she continued talking to Mrs. Payne. "Why are you finding a cook this way and not simply hiring a service to find them?"

"I wanted to see how someone faired before hiring them. You can have a long list of what you've done, where you've cooked, and how many degrees you have. But when it comes down to it, I still have no idea if you can put together a sandwich." Mrs. Payne laughed. "And we got to see that you can indeed do that. Where did you get the mustard you put on the beef? That was the best I've ever tasted."

"I made it. If I don't get the job, then I'll make sure you have the recipe. It's really easy." The timer went off just as she stirred the green beans. "It's show time. If you guys will come on in, we'll see if I can fry up a bird too."

Because they were all eating in the kitchen, Kennedy simply put things on the end of the butcher block as she decanted them and they put them on the table between them. The beans were draining in the sink as she finished putting the chicken on the three platters. When she put the beans into a serving bowl, Butler came around to help her by cutting up the cornbread and putting it in a basket with a towel. Cole slaw was unearthed from the fridge, as well as sliced tomatoes she'd found in the veggie drawer. By the time the last bowl was put on the table, the staff and Mrs. Payne were piling their plates. Kennedy was wiping down her knives to put into her case when she heard someone call her name.

"You'll join us, won't you?" Kennedy shook her head and reached for her coat as Butler looked at Mrs. Payne. "I'm hoping you will. It would be an honor to have you eat with us."

She started to tell him no, that she really needed to get back. They'd assured her that she didn't have to clean up, but she'd done most of that while she worked. When Caroline and the others started nodding for her to join them, she put her coat on the chair again and went to join them.

"I can't eat too much. I have a long night ahead of me and I don't want to fall asleep too early." Potatoes and corn were passed to her as she put smallish portions on her plate only to have Brigitte put more on it. "I don't eat that much in a week."

"Learn to deal with it." Brigitte laughed when she did. "I cannot tell you the last time I had better cornbread. It's almost like a sweet cake."

"Thank you," Kennedy said, blushing. "I learned that from my *seanmháthair*, my grandma. She was a big fan of cornbread, and I wanted to please her with it. It was on my final at college and I got extra marks for it."

Dinner was a hit if the cleaned platter and bowls were any indication. The last piece of chicken was wrapped in a paper towel for "later," Mrs. Payne said as she wrapped up the last piece of cornbread as well. Kennedy started to help clear when she was asked to have a seat.

"We have one more candidate. She comes in tomorrow." Mrs. Payne handed her a sheet of paper, and Kennedy looked down at it. "Do you know how to make those dishes?"

"Aye." Kennedy realized that she'd slipped, but was looking hard at the list and didn't care. "There are things on here that I've done before, others I've made once, but just a few I've never encountered. It doesn't mean I canna make them."

"I need to make sure that when we entertain, we're entertaining with the best possible. I know that you won't cut corners when it comes to feeding us, but will you if there are seven hundred people here?" Kennedy looked at the list again before answering her.

"You get me the ingredients I ask for without cutting corners on your end and I won't either. If you ask me to make you baked salmon from Alaska, then getting me something off the coast of Florida won't do. Understand?" They all three nodded and smiled. "I canna abide by people moving things in my kitchen either. I put it somewhere, that's where I expect to find it when I go back for it. And no one touches my knives."

"My mate does that," Brigitte said with heat in her voice. "Moves things to suit him when it's my kitchen. I've a mind to bash his head in at times when he does it. Just last week it took me hours to find my measuring spoons. We nearly didn't have dinner because of it."

Brigitte nodded as she glared at her husband. The two of them were the cutest couple she'd ever seen and would bet her last nickel that he might move things where she didn't want them just to see the fight in her eyes. Mrs. Payne pushed a second sheet of paper toward her, and Kennedy looked at it quickly before looking back at her.

"We'd like for you to fill this out. It's the application we're saving for the person who gets the job. If the person tomorrow is the dud I've heard he is, then I'd very much like for you to start as soon as possible." Kennedy nodded and tried her best to keep the excitement out of her voice.

"I'm thinking I'd like to dance a jig, but I won't." She picked up the paper and held it as still as she could. "I'll not disappoint you, Mrs. I swear I will give you what I have and then some."

"We know that. I just wish I'd not set up the appointment for tomorrow now. I would love to find out what you'd have in store for us in the morning for breakfast."

Kennedy went back to her camper and emailed her *seanmháthair*. There was one from her, and after reading it twice, Kennedy decided that she'd better take some extra precautions. Her brother had found out she was in the States. Not where yet, but he would. Pulling the heavy blanket over her, Kennedy thought of her brother and decided that she might get herself a ball bat. She'd heard they were very helpful in these sorts of situations. She just hoped it didn't come to that.

Chapter 3

The drive took him over nine hours, and he was now on the last hour of it. Samuel was exhausted and just wanted to crawl into his bed and sleep for the next five years. He turned the radio up louder as he drove down the highway. Christ, he should have waited until morning.

But he wanted to get home. Something was driving him to get there, and as soon as the meeting was over on Thursday at five o'clock, he finished packing up his things from the hotel and checked out. He was hoping to be home by five in the morning.

He was finished with Illinois. And now he had a fat bank account to show that hard work did really pay off. Samuel was looking forward to running in the backyard, sleeping until he wanted to get up, and doing some of the things he'd not done because he'd been too busy focusing on his business. But as Aggie had told him several times, he was leaving it in good hands. His phone ringing startled him.

"How close are you?" His mom sounded as tired as he was. "I can't sleep until you're home and not out on some deserted road. When you get here, I'll sleep."

"I'm almost there. I had to make a couple of stops on the way, but I should be pulling up in front of the house in less than an hour." He laughed. "Mom, you do know that I'm thirty-two years old, right? And I've been driving myself for a long time as well."

"Don't be smart. I know how old you are. And that does not negate the fact that you're still my son and I worry about you. Now, tell me what you're planning to do tomorrow. Any women involved in your life that I should know about?" He knew she was kidding him, but he still squirmed on his seat. "Samuel?"

"I'm here. And no, there isn't any woman in my life. And you know as well as I do that it's not going to happen for me either." Samuel heard her heavy sigh. "I'm sorry, Mom. I know you had your heart set on grandchildren, but I just…there are too many things that could go wrong that I don't want to have to deal with. Too many…everything."

"Samuel, not all mates are like your father. Look at you, you're as different to him as night and day. You might just be surprised at what happens when someone comes into your life." He snorted. "She may be right around the corner from you. You never know."

"It doesn't matter to me if she's living in my house right at this moment, I don't want anything to do with women long-term. I know you've heard me say this before, but I don't want a mate, not now, not ever." Samuel wished now he'd not answered the phone but knew that she'd only call him back over and over until he had. "Mom, don't try to set me up. I don't want it."

"All right. I won't. But I don't have to like it." He heard her saying something to someone and wondered who else was up. "Kennedy just got here. She's going to fix you some breakfast and then go back home."

"That's not necessary." He wasn't hungry, but when his mom insisted, he told her just to make sure it was light. "I don't want anything heavy on my belly when I go to bed."

"I understand. She said she can do that." His mom spoke again, and this time he heard the other voice. She was saying that light was for wussies and his mom laughed. For some reason that pissed him off, and before he could think he was simply too tired to keep his mouth shut, he asked to speak to her.

"You will know that I am far from a wussy, Miss Buehler, and you'll learn your place or find employment elsewhere. When speaking to my mother you'll treat her with respect or I'll show you how protective I can be with what's mine." She didn't say anything, and he was afraid she'd hung up on him. He was ready to check his phone when she spoke.

"You think to threaten me, do ye? Well, I've news for you, boy-o. I've been beaten by the worst of them and come out on top. Aye, more'n on top if you ask me. You keep your tongue behind your teeth or I'll put so much soft peter in your meal that that you'll be a begging me to stop." He heard his mom's sharp intake of breath, but the girl wasn't finished. "Ye overbearing pisser. I should have.... You can go to hell, you rotter."

This time there was no doubt that she'd hung up. She'd slammed the phone down so hard on that he felt the ringing in his ears all the way to his toes and back. When he started to redial his home to speak to her again, fire her he supposed, his phone rang in his hand. Before he could speak, his mom tore into him like he was five and had dug up all her flowers to have himself a bit more land to play in.

"What is wrong with you, young man? Did I not teach you better manners than to threaten someone? What is wrong with you?" He started to tell her that the girl had started it when his mom spoke again. "I'll have you know that we'd been talking about you all day yesterday, and I told her that you'd been a good and kind child and had grown up to be a better man. I even went so far as to tell her I was never more proud of you than when you treated the people who worked for you with respect and goodwill, and now you do this? I'm mortified."

"She called me a wussy." As soon as the words were out of his mouth, he realized how ridiculous it sounded. Like he was a little boy and was insulted by the class bully. "Mom, I'm really tired. Tell her that I'm sorry and that—"

"You'll tell her, not me. You'll come right into this house and you're going to beg her to forgive you." She huffed at him again. "If I let you into this house. Samuel James Payne, I'm embarrassed at your behavior."

Samuel pulled over to the side of the road. He was exhausted, and now he was pissed. This was no way to drive, so he took several deep breaths before he spoke again. He hated to upset his mom more than anything in the world.

"I'm going to be home in about forty minutes. I just want to come into the house and go to my bed. I'll be able to deal with her when I get up. I'm sorry I embarrassed you. I should have kept my mouth shut. I'll make it up to both of you." He only hoped he could. His mom was really pissed off. "I'm terribly sorry, Mom."

"You shouldn't have said anything to her. She's come in on her day off to cater to you." He thought he couldn't have felt any worse, but he did. "What with her having a cold and all, she'll still come in to fix you a breakfast."

"Tell her I'm sorry and I'll pay her for her time." He wondered how much he was paying her and thought about doubling her pay, but his mom spoke up first.

"I'll let her go home after she feeds the rest of us. She's already started cooking." He heard the others in the room now and smiled when Butler greeted everyone in his booming voice. "I'm still upset with you."

"I know and I'm very sorry." He pulled back into traffic after hanging up the phone and thought about how badly he'd screwed up. Next time he had to come this far he was taking a plane. He would have been there by now and all cozied up in his bed. The last five miles seemed to be the longest of the entire trip.

~~~

Kennedy pulled the last of the trash out of the bathroom and took it to the dumpster. It hadn't occurred to her to make sure that her trash was at the site before now. And the trash company was really nice in waiting for her. Normally someone came by and picked up the trash right outside the sites when there had been guests in the place, but she'd completely forgotten.

"There you be, miss. All fixed up." The man took the bag from her and dropped it into the back of his smelly truck. "I'll be here every other Tuesday through the winter months. If you need more of a pickup, just holler and I'll come by." She nodded at him.

"Thanks so much again for waiting on me." She pulled her coat tighter around her, thinking that it was fucking cold out and this man was standing in only his shirt sleeves. "I'll remember from now on."

He was gone ten minutes later, and she made her way back to her home. There was a lot to be said for being waked up at three in the morning by someone pounding on your door. At least he'd not said anything when she answered the door with a ball bat over her shoulder. Going inside, she tried to get warm by dancing around the tiny space, but only made a breeze around her feet. Getting back into the bed, she covered up with every blanket she owned and still couldn't get warm.

"No hope for it, Kennedy dear, might as well get your butt rolling and get to work." She gathered up her things and took them to the bathhouse. Turning the water as hot as she could get it, she stripped down and waited for the steam to warm up the tiny room. She was washing her hair when she thought of Mr. Payne.

For some reason she'd expected his voice to be softer. Mrs. Payne, Summer as she'd asked Kennedy to call her, told her that her son was a great man. Kennedy didn't think much of the man right now and didn't particularly want to meet him either. But today he was going to have breakfast with the staff and apparently tell her how sorry he was. She was glad now that she'd not told anyone but her *seanmháthair* that she'd gotten this job. She might just be out of work by the end of the day.

Her car started with its usual moans and groans. She knew that she needed to get it in for repairs, but the money that she was saving didn't include a thousand dollars to some guy who thought he might be able to fix it. She was going to take her chances with sweet talking it. When it finally rolled over she patted the dashboard as she put it into gear. Time to get moving.

No one was in the kitchen when she got there. They'd given her a key a few days ago when she'd had to wait in her car for the household to open up. Summer had told her she could come and go as she pleased, but Kennedy didn't really think she meant coming over for a barbeque or a dip in the indoor pool. So she started getting things set up just as the sun was rising.

There were cinnamon rolls still proofing on the counter when Butler and Brigitte came in the room. Nodding to them, she continued to knead bread that she was preparing for dinner tonight, and if she was still there after the meeting, she was making a standing rib roast, apparently the lord of the house's favorite.

Kennedy had taken to calling him that under her breath since he'd pissed her off. She was pretty sure that Summer knew she did it, but other than laugh a few times when Kennedy had said it, Summer had said nothing else. By the time breakfast was ready to be served, the table had been set and coffee was brewing. She looked up when the door opened again, thinking it was Butler coming back for more platters.

The master of the house wasn't at all what she'd expected him to look like either. She had no idea what she'd thought, but this man, this gorgeous hunk of a man, was no way near it. When she swallowed twice she had a feeling he knew she'd been struck dumb when he laughed. Turning away from him before she did something incredibly stupid like ask him if she could nibble on him, she picked up the last of the food and took it past him into the dining room.

He touched her arm and stopped her. "I'd very much like a word with you before we eat. It's about the last night."

"I've a breakfast to put on the table, if you don't mind." Her voice was sharper than she'd meant it to be, and his raised brow told her he'd noticed it too. "Ye make me nervous. I'm a wee bit afraid of saying the wrong thing."

"You're Irish." She nodded, embarrassed now that he'd think she was daft too. "My mother said that I needed to apologize to you before we ate."

"Ye mother? Ye not be doing this on yer own then." She pulled from his hand, moved back into the kitchen, and slammed the platter down. "Ye be not wanting to piss off yer mother, so you come to do her bidding no matter what."

"That's not what I meant. I only meant that she suggested that I apologize to you. I upset her when I was rude to you." He looked at the door as it opened and handed the platter to Brigitte and asked for a few minutes. "I didn't mean to insult you. I was tired and I said some things I shouldn't have."

"Aye you did. To me." She started for her coat, knowing that if she didn't leave now her temper was going to explode. But he grabbed her again.

"Wait a damned minute. I'm trying to make this right. Why don't you get your panties out of the twist you have them in and cut me some slack? I'm trying to do the right thing here." She jerked from him again only to have him push her against the wall. Kennedy lost what little control she had on herself and hit him.

She'd never understand if she lived to be three hundred years old how she ended up over him when he'd fallen. Her body lay sprawled all over his in a way that she could feel every hard muscle of his entire frame, and there wasn't any doubt to her that he was all hard muscle. When she tried to scramble off him he put his hands on her hips and held her still. His cock seemed to grow as she lay there.

"You've got blood on your lip." His voice was husky and soft. She licked it off and tasted the copperiest of it. "You okay otherwise?"

"Fine." This time when she tried to get up he groaned deep in his chest and she felt it along her breast. There was something very appealing about him making noises, she thought. Making sure she didn't elbow or knee him again, she stood up and moved her back to the door. As he stood, she had a sudden thought that he was going to hit her back, but he only grinned at her.

"You've a hell of a left. Did it hurt your hand?" She looked down at the bruising already starting to appear. When she tried to put it behind her he asked to see it.

"I'm peachy, thanks." But he pulled her arm toward him and then her hand. When he turned it over in his big palm she felt the air in her lungs rush out. Her hand was so much smaller than his.

"You'll need to put some ice on it." She looked up at him and wondered about the anger she heard. Sure she'd hit him, but he'd been okay with it until now. "Then I'd very much like to have a conversation with you."

"I need to get going, maybe some other time." She went to the refrigerator. After pulling out a zip baggie, she started to fill it with ice only to have him push her out of the way and do it himself. She was getting angrier by the minute. The man ran as hot and cold as the shower where she was staying.

"I shouldn't have yelled at you." His back was to her, but she heard him just fine. "I was tired and out of sorts, and I shouldn't have taken my mood out on you."

He turned to her then and handed her the ice. He was saying the right words, but they weren't sincere sounding. Instead of pointing this out to him, she simply nodded. Tomorrow she'd give her notice. She would not work for this man.

Saying nothing to him, she passed him and went into the dining room. They were all talking until that moment, and she tried not to be hurt by it. Instead, she sat down at the table and put a roll on her plate. Kennedy wasn't sure she could even get that down, but she had to have something on her plate. Mr. Payne came in a few seconds later and sat at the head of the table. Kennedy tried her best to ignore him.

"I wanted to tell everyone welcome. In the coming months I'll be getting used to being idle and trying to stay out of your way." Kennedy could feel his eyes on her, but she didn't raise her head. Picking up her fork, she stabbed at the confection until she was sure it resembled a pile of mashed potatoes. Putting down her fork, she looked down at her hands until she heard someone say her name. Looking up, she realized that Mr. Payne had apparently said it a few times, because they were all grinning at her, with the exception of him.

"I'm not sure what you want from me as a cook. I'll make whatever meals you want. Just leave me a note on the counter." Not that she'd be there much longer, but she wouldn't go out with them thinking she didn't do her job.

"I was asking for you to tell us about yourself. I know you have a bit of Irish in you. I've heard it along with some of your temper." She flushed hotly at him and he grinned. "Ms. Buehler and I have some things to work out."

"Aye we do." She looked around the table before she continued. "I'm Kennedy Buehler. I've lived in the States for nine months now, though I was born here. My family resides in Ireland with my mother and *seanmháthair*. I studied at the Le Cordon Bleu College in Paris before finishing my education at Harvard, where I studied Business Law. I speak nine languages including Gaelic, and I have a black belt in karate."

She'd not meant to tell them all that. It had been too much. She could see that now. She and Mr. Payne stood at the same time and moved to the door. There was no way she'd talk to him now. He'd tell her she was a showoff and a bitch for saying those things, just as her brother had.

"Wait. Christ, why are you always in such a hurry to leave here?" She turned to look at him as she wrapped her knives up and shoved them into her pocket. "You didn't tell my mother that, did you? You didn't mention any of your education to them."

"I applied for the job as they instructed. I didn't fill out the application until after she'd told me I'd had the job." Lifting her chin, she glared at him. "I'm not stupid."

"No, I'd say you're far from that." He sat down on the stool on the opposite side of the bar from her. "Please have a seat. We really should try to start over."

"I…you're not going to hit me?" She flushed when she said it, and when he looked at her with narrow eyes, she decided that she'd really like to see Shamus tangle with this man. He'd learn a thing or two about hurting someone. Kennedy perched on the edge of the other stool

"Who hit you?" He said it low, but there was a good deal of steel in his voice. "Tell me. I'll make sure he doesn't do it again."

The hair on the back of her neck danced, and she suddenly decided that she wouldn't piss this man off again. If he did decide to hurt her, he'd more than likely kill her. Instead of answering him, she changed the subject.

"I'm giving my notice tomorrow." He shook his head. "I canna work for you. You're…you and I will never get along and I don't want to upset Summer. I like her and the rest of your staff."

"Meaning you don't care for me." She didn't answer him, and he threw back his head and laughed. Her entire body went on alert, and she found that she wanted to hear him do that again. Before she could act on that, she stood up again. "Please sit down. I'm not pissed at you. I'm…few people stand up to me. And fewer still hit me on first acquaintance. Please?"

She sat down. "I believe you're a mite nuts." He stared at her for several seconds. It was as if he was looking for something. When he stood up and walked behind her, she tried her best not to squirm, but when he touched her ponytail and moved her hair out of the way of her neck, she shivered. His hot breath on her neck was all the warning she had before he licked her. Kennedy moaned before she could think not to, and when he stepped back from her, she found she wanted to reach for him to…she wasn't sure what she wanted him to do, but it wasn't going to happen.

"You'll stay here so that I can keep an eye on you. And we, you and I, will avoid each other at all costs. Do you understand?" He was breathing hard, and his voice had turned hard again. When she stood up, he backed from her as if she was going to hurt him. "Stay away from me and we'll be just fine."

With that he turned and left the room. Kennedy sat down hard on the stool again and tried to think what the hell just happened. The man was nuts, certifiable, as a matter of fact. She decided that she was going to find something else, and as soon as she did, she was out of there. This place was insane.

Chapter 4

Samuel went to his office and closed and locked the door. Christ, she was his mate. Leaning heavily against the door, he closed his eyes while he tasted her again on his tongue. Whatever had possessed him to taste her was beyond him, but now it was too late to take it back. She was as much a part of him now as she'd ever be. Because as surely as he was standing there, he was not taking this any further with her.

Going to his desk, he found her application on the top of a pile of mail. He read over every line until he got to her signature on the last page. Her education was exemplary and a good deal more than she'd said at the table.

He'd no doubt that had he not pissed her off no one would have known about her background unless they picked up her application and read it. Samuel had a feeling that she'd only said it then to show him she really wasn't stupid. Why she'd thought she had to explain that to him was obvious. He'd been an ass to her and she fought back the only way she could. He rubbed his jaw, thinking she did have a nice hook.

Samuel logged into his computer and decided to do a quick background check on the girl. Not that he thought he'd find anything wrong, but he wanted to find out who had hit her. When he put a search in for her name, he got immediate hits. Christ, she was famous.

At the age of seventeen she'd entered the college, already having worked at some of the most prestigious restaurants across Europe. Article after article about her told of her expertise in putting together meals fit for kings and queens, as well as doing it for soup kitchens and homeless shelters. Kennedy Buehler was not a household chef. He wondered why she was working for him and not some five-star restaurant. Digging deeper, he thought maybe he found out why. Samuel called a friend of his.

"I need you to do some checking for me," he told his good friend, James Burger. He gave him everything he had on her, including her social security number.

"How deep you wanting me to go this time? All the way to how much she weighed at birth, or just enough so her family will stop hounding you to marry her?" There was a good deal of humor in Jimmy's voice, and Samuel realized that he'd had him do this numerous times before.

"All of it. And there's no marriage in mind with this woman. She's my chef. And for your information, she doesn't care for me overly much." That made his friend laugh even harder. "This isn't funny, you moron. I think the woman is my mate, and I want to figure out who the hell hit her."

That shut him up. The silence was so profound that Samuel had a moment to wonder if Jimmy would come over just to ask him if he'd heard him right. When he spoke this time it was with caution.

"What are you going to do now?" Jimmy knew his aversion to having a mate. Hell, the man had as much reason to distrust the whole thing as he did. But his had been because of another woman; Samuel's was because of his own parents.

"Nothing. She's human, so she has no idea what she is to me, and I've told her to stay away from me. I know that for the long term that's not going to work, but it'll give me time to figure out what to do with her." Samuel knew he was playing with fire having her so close, but he was a bigger man than this and thought he could handle it.

"I don't think this is such a good idea. You're going to take her, and after that, it's going to be all downhill afterwards. You should kick her to the curb now and be done with her." Samuel wanted to agree with him, but something about her made him think she needed protection from someone. "Let me take her somewhere for you. I can find her a job that'll—"

The growl slipped from his lips before he could stop it. Jimmy wasn't a lion like him, but he was a shifter. Wolves were just as territorial as he was. When he didn't say anything more, Samuel did.

"Just find out what you can about her. Everything. I know that she has family in Ireland, so maybe you should start there. It might be nothing at all, but she had an abusive dad, and he's not in the picture any longer." Jimmy said he'd get back with him soon.

Samuel tried to bury himself in the files on his desk. He took three calls from Lilly and then one from Aggie. Things were going well, but there would always be things he knew more about than they did. Lilly asked him if he'd thought about finding a replacement for her yet when she called him this last time.

"You're going to stay there?" She told him she was thinking about it. "You know that I need you, but I can understand why you'd want to stay there. Family and all."

"I like Aggie. He's a good man and is trying very hard to make this work. And I think he will." She laughed a little. "Of course he's not you, but no one can be you."

"Damned right." He told her to stay. "That way if I need for you to stop at the Crumbled Muffin you can bring me my favorite."

There had been a brisk knock at his door cutting off the conversation with Lilly as he had to unlock the door. His mom and Butler stood there, and he had a feeling this wasn't going to be good.

"Did you know that there is a garden in the back of the kitchen?" His mom moved into the room as she continued. Samuel adjusted the chairs so that she was sitting across from him as Butler had. "Kennedy wants to know if it's possible to have it redone so that there are fresh herbs for the kitchen. She said she'd do all the work."

For a second he wondered why she wasn't asking him, then remembered what he'd told her. He glanced at the doorway, wondering what she was doing. His mom cleared her throat.

"I don't care if she wants to work in the garden. If her meals for the rest of her life are anything like the one we had this morning, I'd be fine with whatever she wanted." He flushed a little, thinking of all the things he could give her. "Just tell her to have someone get on it when it's feasible."

"She's upset with you." He didn't say anything to his mom when she said that, but waited for her to continue. "What did you do to her?"

"Nothing. She and I had a disagreement and she stood up for herself. I shouldn't have grabbed her arm." He flushed when his mom raised her brow at him in that *you'd better explain that* sort of way. "She was leaving, and I didn't think it was such a good idea. She punched me in the mouth."

Butler laughed but quickly turned it into a cough when he looked at him. When he cleared his throat for the third time, Samuel took pity on him and laughed too. He told them she had a great left and that he would know better than to tangle with her again.

"See that you don't. I've made her a list for dinner's this week from the one she'd given me. It's only for dinners because I wanted her to have fun with lunch. She said that she'd make breakfast for the staff from now on as well." He took the list and barely glanced at it. "We're having standing rib roast for dinner tonight."

His mouth watered. Christ, he'd not had that since...hell; he couldn't remember when the last time it had been. When he handed the list back to his mom, she told him to keep it. Butler moved out of the room when one of the maids came looking for him. Samuel looked at his mom when she didn't say anything.

"You will stay away from her." He nodded. "She told me that you and she had an agreement. Would you like to share that with me?"

"No." He knew that if he told his mom that Kennedy was his mate that she would stop at nothing to get them together. As it was now he wasn't sure having her in the same house with them was a good idea. But if he stayed away from her, they should be able to work this out until he could—could do something. Samuel had a feeling he was so fucked.

"I see." Samuel was pretty sure she did too. Maybe not that Kennedy was his mate but that he was going to avoid her. He decided that he had to do something sooner rather than later. She left him to his work an hour later after going over some of the things that needed his attention.

His phone ringing startled him. Samuel glanced at his watch and couldn't believe that he'd been sitting there for over two hours. His screen had since gone black, and the coffee he'd brought in here with him was cold as ice. He answered the phone after the fourth ring.

"I didn't think you were going to be there." Jimmy sounded excited. "Christ, do you have any idea who you have working in your kitchen? Damn man, I might come over for dinner every night just to taste her food. She's fucking famous."

"I knew that much, you idiot. I meant for you to find out something about her family." Samuel became aware of the scents coming from the hall and into his office. "I can smell the standing rib roast she's making now. I think she used fresh pepper."

He was teasing his friend and laughed when he whimpered. When he invited him for dinner the man nearly screamed out that he'd be there. Then he grew more serious.

"She's not just this fabulous cook, but she's also from a very wealthy family. Her grandmother is Lady Danielle Kennedy Buehler. Her son, who passed away about four years ago, managed to bring the family fortune from near ruin when he was just a teenager. They're not where they were when the family was in its heyday, but they were doing great until his death." Samuel heard him shuffle papers around before he continued. "Kennedy's father died, and things went back down almost immediately. The oldest son, Shamus, has a bit of a problem. He's not very smart when it comes to investments, and the fucking fool gambles a great deal. I'm looking now, but I think he's into a shark for quite a bit. The family, Kennedy's mother and siblings, will be out on their ass if something doesn't change soon."

"And the grandmother? I take it she's not letting the grandson handle her money." Jimmy said she wasn't. "Smart woman. And what have you been able to find out as to why Kennedy is here?"

"She's engaged." Samuel felt his lion roar against his skin. She was his. Samuel wanted to go and find Kennedy and shake her until she told him what the fuck she was doing here if she was slated to be married when Jimmy continued. "Apparently she isn't too thrilled with her brother's choice of husbands for her either. The man is nearly twice her age and sickly. I'm not sure I'd want my sister marrying him, and I don't care for her."

"So it was arranged." Jimmy told him from what he could find it was. "Let me guess, he's got money and is willing to leave it all to Kennedy in the event that they marry. That brother of hers is a peach."

"You don't know the half of it. The guy I contacted in Ireland said that her brother is a pervert too. I've not been able to narrow that down, but I'm thinking he's gay. Not to say that there's anything wrong with that, but different strokes for different folks. He's been known to…let's just say that he's less than discreet with his affairs. And with the money he owes on top of everything else, Shamus is having a hard time making ends meet. The way he's trying to bring things together is by gambling more and more. Idiot."

Samuel wondered aloud what the hell he was doing arranging a marriage for his sister. "I mean, you should see her. Blazing red hair, skin the color of peaches, and freckles that seem to get darker when she blushes. And Christ, a body that would make a monk whimper." He knew that he'd said too much when Jimmy didn't comment. "I won't touch her."

"I would say something glib, but you'll take back your invite to dinner. Samuel, she's going to get you trapped up if you don't watch yourself. She's going to be your mate if you keep thinking of her like that."

"No, she won't. I won't allow it." Samuel glanced up when someone went by the door and it was her. "She's not going to trap me."

He got up after hanging up to close his door...or at least that was his intention. Instead, he found himself following her scent until he found her. She was in the living room speaking to Caroline.

"I don't want to miss. You should ask one of the others to do it." Caroline looked around the room and spotted him in the doorway before he could move. "There's Mr. Payne now. You go ahead and ask him."

Caroline took off out of the room like he'd shot her from a cannon. Kennedy started after her when he asked her what she needed. He could tell she was upset, but unless she told him what it was, he couldn't fix it for her. Samuel asked her what she needed.

"My car won't start." He nodded as she continued. "I need to get to the store for something, and I don't have a way to get there."

"What is it you need? Perhaps I can send Butler after it." She turned a bright red and told him it was personal. Samuel had to hide a grin. The woman was absolutely adorable.

"I just need some shampoo and stuff. I'm not sure what you're thinking, but it's not that personal. It'll be too late when I leave here and I don't have anything for tomorrow." She moved to the door, and he felt his lion stir. She was forever running from him.

"I can take you." The words were out before he could think not to say them. But when she looked at him suspiciously, he knew he had to take her now. "Get your coat and we'll go now if you have time."

"I thought I was supposed to stay away from you. Isn't that sort of defeating the purpose if you take me in your car?"

He didn't care for her tone or what she was saying, and it made his temper short.

"Get your coat. I don't want you coming here tomorrow smelling bad and making the meals you cook off." She moved past him, and he heard her mumble something. He'd heard what she'd said but asked her to repeat it.

"I said that's the man I know. You're a prick, did you know that?" When she made to slip past him, he reached for her. When her body was slammed into his, Samuel pulled her closer until she was flush with him. Then he pulled her mouth to his.

~~~

Kennedy was stunned when he pulled her so close to him. But as soon as he kissed her, she felt everything in her turn to mush. The man could kiss like no one she'd ever been kissed by before. When he lifted her up so that her feet no longer touched the floor, she felt her legs being lifted so that she was wrapped around him.

The wall pressing behind her made her moan. He was lifting her even higher now until his hard cock was between her folds. She pulled her mouth from his and threw back her head. Christ, he was going to make her come. When his mouth opened over her pounding pulse, she wrapped her hands into his hair and held him to her. She had no idea what he was going to do, but she wanted it all. His grinding hips made her wet with need.

"I want to taste you." Kennedy nodded at his harsh words. "I need to taste you, please. Come for me. Come, Kennedy."

Her body didn't just respond to his words but seemed to detonate with his command. As soon as she cried out her release, she felt his teeth scrape against her throat, then a hard pinch as he bit her. She came again, this time crying out his name over and over as he suckled at her neck. When he raised his head and looked at her, she could feel his eyes burn into her before he licked at her throat again. He held her against the wall for long moments while she tried to think what to do now.

"You didn't stay away from me." He lifted his head again and glared at her. "Do you have any idea what you just did?"

"I did?" He nodded and set her on her feet and took a step back, which she thought was very smart on his part since she wanted to tear his throat out. "I was leaving the room, and you pulled me to you and kissed me."

"You didn't fight me." She looked at him incredulously. "You should have put up more of a fight than letting me nearly fuck you against the wall. And now it's too late."

She slapped him. When he reached for her again, she moved so that her body hit his, and she took him to the floor. Her booted foot was at his throat before he could move. Kennedy looked down at him, furious with the tears that streamed down her face.

"Touch me again and I'll kill you." She put just a little more pressure on his throat before she moved off him and out of the room. Kennedy heard him roar, and she picked up her speed, trying to get out before he retaliated and hurt her. She was nearing the kitchen door when he caught her. She started hitting him until he pulled both her arms above her head and held her.

"Calm down, damn it." She stilled but wouldn't look at him. The tears were making her more pissed at herself than she was at him. "Look at me."

"Let me go." He told her to look at him again, and she closed her eyes. "I want to leave here I doona want to stay here. Yer hurting me."

He backed off from her body and his grip on her hands, but he didn't let her go. Kennedy wiped her tears on her outstretched arm but still wouldn't look at him. When he pulled her chin around with his free hand, she tried to pull away, but he was a good deal stronger than her.

"Did I hurt you?" he asked her again and she finally shook her head. "I'm going to let you down, but please don't leave. For as much as I'd like to let you go, I can't. Not anymore."

When he let her go, she thought about leaving, but he blocked the door. She was trapped, and they both knew it. When he asked her to go to his office, she moved ahead of him toward a room she'd never been in before.

"I'm not sure what you know about us, so I'm going to be honest with you." He sat down at his desk when she sat in the chair across from him. When his mom came into the room as well, Kennedy had the feeling that whatever was going on was not going to be anything in her favor.

"Hello, dear. Are you all right?" Kennedy nodded at Summer. "I'm not sure what's going on, but Samuel here says it's time you know what we are."

"Lions," Kennedy said. "They both looked at her, shocked. "I told you I wasn't stupid. I've known since before I started working here. The people I work for are bears. They told me all about other...creatures here."

"Species. We're species, dear, not creatures." Summer looked at her, then her son. "You think she was stupid?"

"No." He lowered his voice when his mom looked at him oddly. "No. I didn't think she was. Christ, why do you always think someone thinks you're stupid? Is it because of your brother?"

Her skin crawled over her, and she stood up. If he knew Shamus, then he could find her. When she moved to the door,

Samuel was suddenly standing in front of her. She backed away from him but put up her hands in defense.

"I won't hurt you. I can't." She snorted. "I promise you that I'll never hurt you. When your boss told you about them, did they tell you what mates were?"

"No. And frankly I doona care either. You tell Shamus I'm not going back. I doona want to marry that mon any more than I want to marry you." She heard Summer's sharp intake of breath but didn't have time to worry with it now. "I've no use for a mon, any mon, especially one older than rocks."

"Good, because you're not marrying him. You're going to marry me."

Chapter 5

"I canna find her, Shamus. Other than her living in the state of Ohio, but she's not to be found." Shamus slammed down the papers he had in his hand and glared at the man in front of him. "She's hiding good this time."

"I want her here. You find her and drag her back." Shamus looked up when his mother entered the room. "I'm conducting business here. Leave me."

She started to move deeper into the room, but he simply raised his hand. They'd learn who was boss here or he'd have to show them again. When she backed out of the room, Shamus felt like he'd won this round but knew there'd be more. His sisters, both of them, were going to heel or he'd show them what his wrath meant.

"Mayhap your mother knows. Or your grandmother. She and Kennedy were close before your da passed." Donald O'Malley was as stupid as he was big. And the man was the biggest man he'd ever encountered. It was why he had him on his side. The added bonus was that he was handsome too.

"Aye, they were, but she tells me she doona know anything." Shamus was sure she was lying, but there was no touching her. His *seanmháthair* held all the money, and as badly as he wanted it, he was afraid of her. She had more

55

friends in higher places than he could ever dream of. "I want you to go to the Americas and find her. You said you had a clue where she be, go and find her."

Donald was shaking his head before he finished. "I canna and you know it. My wife is due any day now, and I've no passport. Even if I did, I canna leave the country, because of the trouble from years ago. I'm ex-con, and you well know it."

Shamus did know it. He was actually the one that had been in trouble with the law but had given Donald enough money to set him up with a nice house and marry the girl he wanted in exchange for Donald taking the blame. The mon had spent five years in prison for him, and Shamus had taken care of his wife whilst he was away.

"Then I'm guessing there's no hope for it. I must go and bring her home." Shamus looked around the office that had been his da's. There was little left to sell off now for cash, and he'd never found his mother's jewels yet. She'd hidden them away just as tightly as Kennedy had herself. This was not the way he'd envisioned his becoming laird of the house. His family was not cooperating the way he'd wanted. And now Kaitlin was acting up when he'd tried to marry her off to Kennedy's groom. He dinna know where she'd hidden herself off to either.

After Donald left, Shamus went to find his mother. She was going to have to tell him where her money and jewelry was or he'd have to hurt her again. Things were coming to a head, and he wasn't going to waste time begging her for information again. He searched the house twice without finding a single person. It took him a third time around to realize that all the staff, few that they were, was gone as well.

The phone was ringing when he entered the office again. He nearly didn't answer it but wanted answers and mayhap this person had some. When he heard his mother's voice at the other end he started snarling at her before he gave her a chance to say a word.

"You'll come back here this minute. I've a need of your jewels to go and bring home that bitch of a daughter of yours. I'm not fucking around anymore with you and the rest of them. Where are you, and where is Kaitlin?"

"We're not returning." He waited for her to continue, and when she didn't, he started to tell her she bloody hell would, but the line went dead. Shamus waited for her to call back or something, then realized that she wouldn't be able to with him holding the line open. As soon as he put it in the cradle, the thing shrilled again, causing him to squeak.

"Mr. Buehler?" Shamus told him that's who he was, and the man laughed. "You have five days, sir, to come up with the past due amount on the house or we foreclose. The amount you must pay the mortgage company is eighteen thousand euro or twenty-three thousand seven hundred seventy-two dollars and sixty cents in dollars. That being said, I hope you don't come up with it. I've a mind to own the house myself."

Shamus sat down hard in the chair. "Five days. That's not possible. I canna come up with that much money. I need more time."

The man laughed. "We've given you more time than we do others of your standing. You have until Monday to come up with the money. We've started the notification of all those concerned."

Shamus didn't get the chance to ask him who was concerned because his mind was wrapped around the five days. By the time he'd gotten around to asking if he could have an extension, the man had hung up on him. Christ, it was worse than he thought. As he cradled the phone again, he wondered who the other concerned might be that he was talking about, but right now he didn't care. He had to come up with some money. Shamus went to his mother's room and found it not just devoid of her but everything, including her bed. When the hell had that happened?

His sister's room, as well as his brother's room, was the same. Nothing, not even a towel left in the hamper. They'd all left him, abandoned him in his hour of need. Shamus sat down on the floor in his brother's room and looked around. That's when he spied the note sitting atop the fireplace mantle.

You're a fuck up. Shamus felt his anger boil over as he continued to read. *You're not only a fuck up, but a royal fuck up. And stupid as well. Mother moved us out on Wednesday. I've no idea when you've read this but I'm guessing it was a long time passed. See, stupid too. Good luck brother dear, I hope you're happy that you've lost our family home. Sincerely, Michael.*

It was Wednesday, but Shamus had a feeling his brother meant last Wednesday. He tried to remember the last time he'd seen Michael and couldn't. Hell, he wasn't even sure when the last time he'd seen a servant was for that matter. He put the note into his pocket and went in search of his grandmother's number. She wouldn't let the house go to someone else.

"I'm sorry, sir, the mistress is out of the house. I do not expect her to return for at least several months. Shall I tell her you called if she could contact the house?" Shamus hung up. Everyone was against him, and he didn't like it.

The money was simply gone. He'd tried to win it back, but nothing was working the way he'd planned. When he started to notice that he was running low, he'd taken measures to have Kennedy marry old man Tailor, but she'd left him and had run off to the United States. Tailor had promised to make Kennedy his heir, but she'd have to give him a son first. As old as the man was, Shamus had doubted his ability to get hard, much less father a child, and had already made plans to have his sister impregnated by someone else to fob the child off as Tailor's, but that had failed as well. Then he'd thought to get his younger sister to marry him, but she, too, had failed him. Shamus just could not understand his family and their unwillingness to help when he needed them.

He called the bank hoping to get someone that would be willing to give him some extra time and maybe a little money to tide him over. The races were starting up tomorrow night again, and he was sure he could win back all he needed and more.

After being on the line for several minutes, he'd been transferred to someone else. When the woman came on the line, she was less than friendly to him, something that bothered him a great deal.

"I've sent you several letters, Mr. Buehler. The bank no longer owns your note. A company in the America's owns it now." She tisked at him. "And your request for funding is not going to happen either. You've overdrawn your account by several thousand dollars now and we'll not be giving you more."

"Now what?" Shamus sat there for a long time before he got up to see what he could do. It was well into night when he stepped out onto the porch and went out to the barn. The horses that belonged to Kennedy were still there, and someone had fed them. He pulled out his cell phone and made nine calls before he was able to find buyers for them all. He had no papers that said they belonged to him to sell, but the man was willing to wait until his sister returned.

Shamus told him that she'd been hurt and he needed to go to her. By morning he was buying a ticket to the state of Ohio, and he was going to find Kennedy if it was the last thing he did.

~~~

Kennedy went to her car, and thankfully, it started right up. She was driving down the long drive from the house thinking about nothing but the road in front of her and the music that blared on the radio. She refused to think about the fact that Mr. Payne thought he was going to marry her.

When she got back to her home, she sat down on the bench and stared at nothing for a long time, trying her best to wrap her mind around everything. Finally getting up, she went to her computer to see if her grandmother was online. She needed her now more than ever. She wasn't there, but there were nine emails from her. Starting at the first one that had come in she started reading. By the time she got to the last one, Kennedy wasn't sure whether she was terrified or excited. Her *seanmháthair* should be in there in the morning.

Glancing at the email that gave her all the details of her flight, she realized her grandmother had indicated multiple people. She wondered who might be coming with her, but only then realized that she didn't care. Her *seanmháthair* would know what to do.

"I'll be marrying you as soon as it can be arranged. I think you should pack your belongings and move in here as soon as possible. If you've a deposit on your place, I'll be more than glad to reimburse you for it." Mr. Payne had gone over the things he thought she should do as if she'd had no choice. "I've marked you, Kennedy, as my mate, and the sooner we get the bonding part taken care of the better for both of us. I've no need for a mate, but now that I've stupidly taken one I will do everything in my power to make you comfortable."

When he'd asked her if she had any questions she'd only shook her head. Then he'd told her to go home and he'd see her in the morning. Kennedy heard his mother yelling at him before Kennedy had gotten out of the house.

Like hell he would.

Marrying a man like Mr. Payne would be like marrying a man like her brother. Shamus and Samuel were cut from the same cloth. Both men were thinking they could rule her, and she wasn't going to let them. Before she knew it, she'd gotten out her stash of money and was counting it. When her *seanmháthair* got here, Kennedy was going to beg her to take her away and never to return. She was sick of America.

It took her less time than she'd thought it would to pack up, but then in a fit of independence, she put it all away again. Kennedy wouldn't run this time. She'd face the man and tell him to fuck off. Putting her cash back, she went to the phone outside the offices of the campground and called the airport to see if the plane her *seanmháthair* was coming in on was on time. Then when she found out when it was, she got into her car and drove the forty minutes to the airport to be there when she came in.

Kennedy was sitting in the lobby settling down to wait the three hours when something touched her mind. When Mr. Payne spoke to her, she stood up looking around for him when he laughed. Christ love a duck, the man was speaking to her.

I'm wondering what has you so upset. She didn't answer him, not sure how. *Just think like you're speaking to me, and I'll hear you.*

I've no reason to speak to you, Mr. Payne. I think you've said enough to me as well. Leave me be. There was laughter, and Kennedy wondered how she knew he was making fun of her and asked him.

I've marked you, as I told you. And because we're mates, we've a bond that allows us to speak to each other as well as feel each other's emotions. At least I can feel yours. You'd have to bite me for the exchange to be complete. Kennedy tried not to think about biting him, but he knew what she'd been thinking. *Come here, Kennedy, and let me show you the wonders of being mated to a lion. Just pack up your belongings and come here to me.*

She ignored him. There was no way she was going to go to him, and she was never going to bite him. When he started sending her thoughts of them in the bed together, she picked out a man that looked nice and imagined him in her bed. Mr. Payne was not amused.

I think you need a lesson in what it means to be owned by a lion. We're very protective, but more so when it comes to jealousy. You'd do well not to tease me in that way.

You'd do well to leave me the fuck alone. I've made my stand on being your mate perfectly clear. I don't want, nor do I need, you any more than you want or need me, Mr. Payne. Kennedy thought about what he'd said to her about all of this. *You should find someone who will do your bidding. I am not that woman.*

You'll listen to me, Kennedy. You know it's for your own good. I'm your mate and as such I demand that you come to me this minute. Or better yet, tell me where you are, and I'll come to you. Kennedy ignored him even when he threatened her with a paddling. She wasn't five, nor was she a doormat.

Kennedy was on edge when her *seanmháthair's* flight was called. She went as far as security would let her and watched as the passengers came toward her. There were so many of them that she thought she'd missed her when she suddenly appeared. It was all she could do not to run past the gates and hug her. When she was standing before her, Kennedy burst into tears.

"Come, child, doona make a scene. We'll go to the hotel and you'll tell me about it." Before she could tell her she would love that, Kennedy was engulfed in a strong set of arms that nearly choked the breath out of her. When she pulled back, she cried again, finding her little brother and sister there as well. Her mother was standing just behind them.

"You've all come? Oh you've no idea—I've needed to see you so badly." She hugged them all several times on the way to the luggage terminal. "You didn't bring Shamus, did you?"

"Nay, he's back home. What there is left of it. The mon has lost it all. Gambling he does, and that's going to be the death of our home." Her mother hugged her tightly. "You've the right of it coming here and getting out. He'd had you wedded and bedded by some mon that would have left you in ruin without a penny to yer name."

"I would have died first than to marry Patrick Tailor. But I don't understand; what do you mean he's lost our home?" Her mother told her in rapid Gaelic what Shamus had done and tried to do. Marry her off was bad enough, but Kaitlin was engaged to someone she loved dearly. And all for her brother's love of money.

Kennedy looked at her *seanmháthair*. The house that they'd grown up in had been in her family for generations…nine if Kennedy had it right. And now Shamus had lost it all. She felt Mr. Payne touch her mind again but didn't answer him. She was too hurt and sad to deal with him again. When they went to the hotel, they all settled into their rooms well enough, and Kennedy ended up in her *seanmháthair's* room resting on the sofa. Kennedy could still feel Mr. Payne in the back of her mind, but she was getting much better at ignoring him.

"You're hurt, my dear, what's happened?" Kennedy sat up on the couch and looked at her *seanmháthair* as she settled in the chair. "Tell me, and we'll fix it together like we used to."

"There's no fixing this for me." She didn't want to tell her favorite person in the entire world that a man she hardly knew wanted to wed and bed her for no other reason than he said he was supposed to. "I'm so glad you're here."

"Aye, I can tell. The sadness in your eyes tells me you're thrilled to death. Tell me, lass, and let me see if it can be fixed or not."

Kennedy told her everything, even some of the things she knew that she'd never share with her mother or sister. Her *seanmháthair* never said much but asked a few questions. And when she was done, she looked at her with concern in her eyes.

"You've a mind to run from this mon?" She nodded, then shook her head. "Very clear you are about him, I can see. What do you want from him, Kennedy? Love? He more than likely will after a fashion, but not if you flee him."

"He's no desire to love me, only keep me in a shell that will kill me. I don't need a keeper, *Seanmháthair*, but he thinks it's in my best interest for him to be mine." Kennedy started to cry again. "I've been marked by him, and now…now he wants me to give up everything I have."

Her *seanmháthair* sat and looked at her for a long time. Kennedy knew her well enough to know that she was thinking. Dani Kennedy Buehler did not make rash decisions. When she stood up, Kennedy felt disappointed. But her *seanmháthair* hugged her tightly.

"I have to think about this a bit more." Kennedy nodded. "You'll sleep here, of course, and then in the morning, we'll go and see this man of yours."

"Nay, *Seanmhàthair*, I've no desire to see him again." *Seanmhàthair* raised her hand. "I doona think he'll be thrilled to see me anyway. I'm supposed to be packing my things and going back to his bed. I've no desire to go from the fire to the frying pan."

"We'll see." Something about the way she said it had Kennedy thinking she might have been better off not telling her *seanmhàthair* what had happened. When she closed the door behind her to the bedroom, Kennedy sat there for long moments trying to think what was going to happen in the morning, and decided that she didn't want to know. But when she stood up, her *seanmhàthair* came to the door and opened it just enough to see her.

"You run and I'll be sorely disappointed in you, my child. This mon will think you a coward as well. Is that what you want?"

"He doesn't want me." Saying it aloud made the pain more noticeable. "I'll not have anyone in my life that feels that way."

The door closed without a word, and Kennedy sat down. There was no hope for it. She'd have to see Mr. Payne in the morning, and her *seanmhàthair* would be there to witness her humiliations as well. Burrowing deep into the couch, Kennedy let the tears flow. She'd have been better off marrying old man Tailor when she'd been told to. At least he wanted her somewhat.

The dream of her da's death came to her again that night. And when that one ended, the one where her brother beat her followed. The pain of what he'd done to her body was nothing compared to the betrayal she felt from him. But hurt her physically he had.

Broken bones were the most of it, but he'd beaten her with her da's belt, the buckle of it tearing into her skin so deeply in places that they'd had to stitch them closed. Walking had been difficult with all the lashes on her legs. Even when she'd left the hospital, she'd still been in pain, broken ribs not quite healed and her head still concussed. Kennedy, in a word, had been a mess. The only way for her to be able to travel had been by boat and with a nurse by her side. She had much to be grateful for from her *seanmháthair*.

But the men in her life, all of them, including her da, had wanted so much from her. All of them were set to hurt her and make her do as they said no matter what she wanted. Kennedy lay there after the dreams woke her and cried more in the darkness. When sleep finally claimed her, she knew that she'd look awful in the morning.

Chapter 6

"Sir, there's a miss on the phone. She wishes to speak to you." Samuel was still trying to find Kennedy, and he didn't have time for calls. "She said that she is Miss Kennedy's grandmother."

Samuel had the call transferred to his office. When he picked up the handset, he waited for several seconds before he pushed the button to answer the call. He had no idea why she'd be calling him, but he had a feeling she was going to tell him that Kennedy had come to her.

After saying hello and his name, the woman launched into why she called. "I've a mind to see you, young man. Today. This morning if it would suit you."

He had a feeling that even if it didn't suit she'd come anyway. "I'm free for the rest of the day. I'm...is Kennedy with you?"

"She is. I have listened to her side of this sordid tale and would like to hear your side. Do you love her?"

"No. I don't want her even to be in my life, but I've taken her as my mate and I expect her to come here. When will she be able to fly back?" The woman laughed. "I assure you that I'm serious in this."

"Aye, I've no doubt that you are. But you'll learn that I am a great deal less intimated by you than she is. And Kennedy isn't intimidated at all." Her laughter reminded him of Kennedy and he realized how little he'd heard it. There was a great deal of her he'd heard little about, and she'd blocked him somehow.

"I asked her to come here today, and she's disobeyed me. How do I protect her if she won't listen to me?" He felt foolish saying this to Kennedy's grandmother, but she only hummed at him. "And now she's in Ireland."

"Nay, she's here with me. We only just arrived last night. Her mother and siblings are with me as well." She sighed heavily, and he waited for her to speak. "Her brother means to hurt her. He'll come for her because he believes her to be his only hope of getting out of the debt that he's in. He's nearly lost their home, my home, and the rest of the family's because of his greed."

Samuel looked down at the notes he'd taken this morning when Jimmy had called him. "He's in debt for more than the land and house is worth, did you know that? As of right now, he's nearly seventy million dollars in debt. The house and the land surrounding it is less than that."

"I've known for some time that he was gambling away the family money but thought he'd stop. But when he hurt my granddaughter so badly that she nearly died, I decided to let him do what he would so long as she was safe. I sent her to the United States for her freedom, Samuel Payne, not to be mated to an overbearing mon that would stifle what she is." Samuel started to deny what she was saying, but she continued before he could. "I've had you looked into as well. I've a good deal more influence and money than you, so I was able to work faster. You're a person who gets things done. Well, so am I. I'd like to make a deal with you. A partnership, so to speak. Are you willing to listen to an old woman?"

"What do you want from me?" She laughed again. "Kennedy is my mate, and there is nothing you can do about that. I'll have her."

"You'll have her if I allow it." The steel there made his lion curl up inside of him. He'd never had that happen before, and Samuel was suddenly very afraid that she'd do just what she said. He had no idea why, but the thought of being without Kennedy in his life suddenly didn't feel right.

"I'll listen to you, but I'd like to know if Kennedy is all right. Last night she was distraught when I spoke to her, and now…now she's blocked me. I don't know how she's done it, but I can no longer reach out to her."

"She's resting now, though I will tell you that's it's not a restful one. Nightmares haunt her, and she is looking like it. Only just an hour ago I think she fell into an exhaustive sleep. She will not be in the best of humor today." Samuel nearly pointed out that she'd not been since he'd met her but didn't think she'd find the humor in it.

"I'll bring her today with me, but you'll keep a civil tongue in your mouth or so help me I'll make your life a living hell. I dinna live this long without a few tricks up my sleeve." He believed her. "Your lovely mother; will she be there as well?"

"If you'd like." Samuel wanted to ask her about the house and how much it meant to Kennedy, but Mrs. Buehler told him she'd be there within the hour. Samuel hung up the phone and tried to think what the hell he'd just gotten himself into. He went in search for his mom to tell her what was going on.

"You think she's going to tell you to leave her alone?" Samuel thought that she could try, but he didn't think it would work. "I feel badly for poor Kennedy. She's been through some tough times."

He nearly pointed out that he had too since taking her as his mate, but again kept his mouth shut. They entered the kitchen together to let the staff know what was going on. As soon as they had things moving in the right direction, Samuel went back to his office. He was thinking he needed to gird his loins.

They arrived by limo within the hour. The driver handed them all out, and his breath caught when he saw Kennedy. She did look terrible, and his lion wanted him to go to her and comfort her. He doubted his beast had been paying attention if he thought that his mate would allow him to comfort her for any reason. Kennedy just didn't strike him as the hugging sort of person. When a second car pulled up behind the limo, he saw his friend Jimmy get out, along with two men he vaguely knew.

"Mrs. Buehler asked for a team of lawyers, and I brought the best." Jimmy hugged him to him with a hardy pat on the back. "I got to see your mate. Christ, you weren't kidding when you said she was beautiful."

Jimmy had joined them for dinner last night. Kennedy had made the roast and left instructions on how to finish it up before leaving. It was as delicious as he'd thought it would be, and Jimmy had begged him to allow him to move in. And the homemade bread she'd made them was better than he'd ever tasted.

"I would like to say that my granddaughter has told me a great many things since yesterday. All of them I believe, but I'd like to hear what you have to say about this affair." Mrs. Buehler nodded in his direction as she continued. "You said you doona want her? Then why do you demand that she come here to be with you?"

"She's my mate." His mom snorted and he flushed. "I know that that sounds like a stupid reason, but she's supposed to balance me. Make me whole. While I felt as if I was doing fine before, I don't want her running into things halfcocked and getting herself hurt. I can protect her, but not when she's not here."

"I see." He doubted that she could see it at all but wisely kept his mouth shut. "You do know that her brother means to marry her off to another man. And when he does, he's a plan to have her get with child by any means possible, including finding someone to do the deed for her husband if need be. Tailor won't leave her his riches if she doesn't give him a child."

Kennedy stood up, but before she could say anything her grandmother raised her hand. Kennedy didn't look as if she was going to sit down, but when she finally did, she turned her back on the room and stared into the fireplace. He wished he could hide away so easily.

"I've asked Mr. Burger to bring a lawyer to go over the contract that I've had my attorney draw up before leaving. He had it delivered to me this morn with your name on it if you're willing to abide by it." Samuel took the sheaf of papers and sat down and started to read them. He looked at Mrs. Buehler when he got to the second page.

"It says here that I'll inherit the properties and manor when I marry Kennedy." Kennedy didn't say anything, but he could see her back stiffen. "I thought they belonged to your grandson."

"Nay, they belong to me as of last evening. And as soon as you wed Kennedy, I'll sign them over to you. All of it." Samuel continued to read, and when he finished it, one of the lawyers cleared his throat.

"I've read over the contract, Mr. Payne, and it's very much in your favor. When you marry Kennedy and consummate the marriage, you'll own it all. There is also a yearly stipend that comes with the land that we can discuss once you've decided that you'll abide by the rules." He handed him another group of pages. "They're all outlined there. Ms. Buehler will also sign off on this one as her name isn't required for the estate and properties."

"Why not?" The younger man looked at Mrs. Buehler, then at Kennedy. "Why isn't her name required on the contract?"

"Because I'm a female and I canna inherit so long as I have a brother or a husband. It's the way that it was set up when the land was purchased." Kennedy moved to the window when she stood up, and he could see how hurt she was. "If my father had had all girls, one of us would have had to marry or all the lands would revert back to the county. And since I have two brothers of age, they can take it from me or, in this case, you if you decide to marry me."

Samuel looked over the contract again. It was a good deal for him. He'd be the laird of the manor, and she'd be his lady. And all for something that was going to happen anyway. Even the rules he'd been given were things that he'd already decided on. Caring for her family, making sure her brother and sister were educated and wed to proper spouses. He was to provide for her mother as well, giving her an allowance to spend as she wanted, as well as a home she could call her own. He must also care for the houses and the adjoining farms. There was a part about horses, but that had been taken out, and he asked about it now.

"Shamus sold them to come here to get Ms. Kennedy." The other lawyer stood up and handed another handful of papers to him. "I've done as Lady Buehler has asked and found the buyer for them, but I'm afraid that several of them have been destroyed. The man who'd bought them wasn't happy to find that they were not of the quality that he'd been promised."

~~~

Kennedy stared out the window at nothing. Snow was coming down now, and its pretty flakes hit the window and melted almost immediately. She thought that by this evening her little home would be covered in snow and she'd have to dig it out. Laughing slightly, knowing that she wasn't going to get to go back, she squeezed her eyes shut against the pain.

"Kennedy?" She turned to look at Mr. Burger. "I think they need you, love. You should go back over so you can hear your fate."

"I know what it is already, sir. It's just a different mon who's going to hurt me." He shook his head, and she nodded. "Aye, we both know that he's no desire to have me any more than I do him. If he doesn't sign the contract, he's a bigger fool than I thought."

"Samuel's no fool, but he might surprise you when it comes to taking care of what's his." Kennedy looked out the window again. That was the problem really, she didn't want to be his or anyone's. When her *seanmháthair* said her name and asked her to look at her; she had no choice. Kennedy respected her *seanmháthair* more than anyone she knew, but Kennedy didn't want this and had told her so.

"You do this, make me do this, and I'll not forgive you." The Gaelic she'd spoken wasn't loud, but she heard her all the same. "I doona want this, and neither does he."

"He's signed the contract, my darling. And the judge here is going to wed you before Shamus can get to you." *Seanmháthair* brushed her fingers against her cheek. "You'll see. He'll come to love you as much as I do."

Kennedy watched as Samuel signed his name to the contract. He looked at her, and she could see the determination in his eyes as well as the steel that he would use to crush her. When everything was witnessed and signed off on as well, Kennedy felt her heart break even more. The deed was done, and she was as good as wed.

"I've a ring that I'd like for you to use if you don't have one from your own mother." Samuel shook his head at his *seanmháthair* question, but continued to look at her. "It's been in my family for generations, seven back from the time we became the owners of Rose Manor."

Kennedy knew the ring. Her *seanmháthair* had worn it all her life and the matching one, her grandda's, hung around her neck on a gold chain. She handed this to Samuel as well. He stared at them both, and when he read what was inside her grandda's ring, he looked at her again.

"You were named for him." She nodded and stood up to go back to the couch. But he asked her what her *seanmháthair's* ring said.

"'Tis Irish. *Beidh mé grá agat go dtí an foircinn am agus go deo níos mó tar éis. It means I will love you until the ends of time and forever more after.*" When he didn't ask her anything else, she sat down. It was something her grandda had said to her *seanmháthair* all her life. And her da to her mom as well.

"The wedding will take place today, if possible." Kennedy turned around to see how that was even possible. But Samuel had it all arranged. "I've contacted a friend of mine, and he's agreed to do the ceremony for us. The license was taken care of yesterday. All it needs is Kennedy's signature."

When she started to protest, her *seanmháthair* looked at her. Snapping her mouth closed, she turned away again. This was going to be the worst day of her life. No one cared that she didn't want this. All they wanted was to get it settled so that they could move on with their lives. Her mother asked her to come and let her help her dress.

"I'll be wearing what I'm wearing. 'Tis not a celebration we're having." Her mother tisked at her. "I agreed to this because I've no choice. You want me to dress in a white gown and play the part of a blushing bride? You can go to hell."

Her mother slapped her. It was no less than she deserved, but still it hurt. She heard Samuel coming toward her, but she didn't acknowledge him either. Her mother turned her back on her and walked away. Samuel jerked her around to face him.

"You plan on pissing everyone off today? It's your wedding day; you should at least be somewhat happy." He glared at her. "You'll be my wife soon, and I'll make sure that your brother never bothers you again."

"Please call this off, Mr. Payne. I beg of you. This isn't right, and you well know it." He tried to pull her closer to him, but she jerked away. "You don't love me any more than I love you."

"No, we don't love each other, but we may soon. When we have children, we'll be happier." When he reached for her again, she could see the anger in his eyes, but he shook it off before he continued. "You'll have to stop calling me Mr. Payne. My name is Samuel, Samuel James Payne."

Kennedy nodded. There was no hope for it. He was going to go through with this, and she wasn't going to be able to talk him out of it. When the judge asked her if she needed to change, she told him no, that she was ready. She glanced at Samuel again as he straightened his tie, but he never asked her to change. She wouldn't have been able to stomach putting on a wedding gown for this, and she was pretty sure he knew it.

In a matter of minutes, they were being pronounced man and wife, and she was wearing the heavy ring that was her *seanmháthair's*, and he was wearing her grandda's. It bothered her so much that the rings fit them as if they'd been made for them. Her *seanmháthair* pulled her aside just after they were presented to those present as husband and wife.

"You'll do as you promised for me." She nodded and tried to pull away, but she held her tight. "A promise is a promise, and you gave me your word."

"I'll not leave him or hurt him. I'll give him my body and whatever he wants." Kennedy pulled her arm free of her *seanmháthair's* grip. "But he'll never have my heart. I'll never love him or want his love in return. I'll be his wife, but I'll never be his love."

She turned to see him standing behind her, and she lifted her chin. If he wanted to hit her for this, she'd welcome it. She was being forced into this to protect her family. Her *seanmháthair* had told her that if she did this, she would make sure that Michael and Kaitlin both would be able to marry someone of their choosing, and they'd be ones that inherited all her *seanmháthair's* fortune.

Chapter 7

Samuel moved through the woods quietly. Not because he felt he had to stalk something. On the contrary, he just didn't want anyone to bother him. There were enough beings out in his woods now that he felt closed in. And he wanted more than anything to be alone.

She'd hurt him. He wanted to think that she'd not meant it, but there was little doubt that she had. And it wasn't as if he loved her either, but she'd been so final about it. As if she'd do everything in her power to make sure she never loved him.

That had cut him as deeply as any wound his father had given him, and his heart still ached from it. Kennedy would never love him, not now and not ever. How could a woman...? Samuel started to say how could a woman say such a thing, but he'd had a talk with her grandmother after she'd left the room, and he could well understand some of her pain. Kennedy had been cornered by all of them.

"I want her safe, not just from Shamus, but from all men. Kennedy had hardened her heart against love. Her parents had never loved each other, but her father loved her. Kennedy was his bright star in a marriage that was full of accusations and cruel words. My son was a good man, but like all people he had his faults. He let Kennedy get her education, but he never took it seriously. When she graduated at the top of her class, he asked her why she had tried so hard to show up the men. He told her that she made it hard for him to find her a husband when she was so much smarter than them. She just laughed at him and told him she was never going to marry." She reached into her pocket and handed him a photo. It was of Kennedy and her parents. They looked as if they'd rather have been anywhere but there. "That was taken the day she graduated with honors from the cooking college she went to."

"She looks…embarrassed. Like she'd rather be elsewhere as well." She took the picture back when he handed it to her. "What happened?"

"You're very smart." Dani laughed a little. "Her father had just told her that she was going to be married. He'd found her someone that would care for her, he'd told her. They fought terribly, and in the end, she ran away. He didn't try hard to find her, but I knew where she was. I think he knew it as well. The day he died was her first week home. They told us that Kendal had a massive heart attack."

"You don't think so." She shook her head. "Christ, you think Shamus did it. You think he killed his own father."

Samuel had listened to her explain that he'd been in very good health. Not only that, but he'd had a physical the week before for insurance and they'd told him he had the heart of a much younger man. She'd asked for a report on his death and was told that his son, the oldest, was in charge now, and he'd had his father cremated.

Samuel hated his own father, but to kill him? He knew that he'd never be able to do anything like that. He was a prick and a bastard, but he was still his father. But that didn't mean that if he drew back his hand to hit anyone, he might not consider killing him. And this included Kennedy now. But poison would have been harsh.

You do know that you've been out here for nearly four hours, don't you? His mother touched his mind gently, but he could still feel that she was upset with him. *Your wife is asleep on the couch in the living room, and all your guests have left. I'd carry her up myself, but you know that's not possible.*

She hates me. His mom told him he was wrong. *No, she does. And I can't blame her. I...everyone in her family from her father to her grandmother have forced her into this situation, and now I have done so as well. She'll hate me for this.*

Come inside and talk to her. She's had a hard time of it and she needs to know that you're not going to hurt her. But he had, and he told his mom he had. *By giving her a life she'd never have? Keeping her from a brother that would harm her...did you know that he beat her? Took a belt to her back so badly that.... Oh Samuel, she needs us.*

He told her he'd be in soon. Samuel was making his way to the house when he saw someone, another lion, coming toward him. He lowered his body to the ground and waited. When he caught his scent, every part of him froze. What the fuck was his father doing there?

Hello, son. Samuel moved forward but not close enough to have his father touch him. He did tell his mom to lock the doors and that he'd explain later.

What do you want here? In the event it escaped your notice, you're not welcome. I'd very much like it if you left.

You have a mate. Samuel glanced at the house, then back at his dad, saying nothing. *I was wondering if I could meet her.*

No. You stay away from my family. His father sat down and snarled slightly. *You were told to stay away from us and never to contact us again. I can only assume you know about the house and land.*

Yeah, that's why I'm here. I want my share. Samuel only stared at him. *I know you sold it off. It's only fair that I get some of that money, if not all of it. I did raise you up in that place.*

And hit mother and I. You made our lives a living hell there, and when you left, you owed a great deal of back taxes as well as several months of back payments to the bank. Samuel glanced at the house when he heard the door open. Butler was on the porch now, and he had a shotgun in his hand. *That man up there knows what to do if you try anything, and when he shoots you, I'm going to piss on your carcass.*

That's no way to talk to your father. I gave you what you are today. Just give me my fucking money, and I'll get out of your hair. Samuel started to move by him when he felt his father move. It only took Samuel a second to turn on him and have him pinned down to the ground in a hold that he'd not break.

I want you to get the fuck off my property. And never return. I'm not giving you one thin dime of the money. Samuel let him go and moved to the house. He didn't want to enter as a lion because the rest of the staff hadn't been made aware of him, but Butler had it covered.

There were clothes just inside the little laundry room, and he shifted quickly and went back out on the deck with just his pants on. His father was still here, but he moved toward the woods when he saw Samuel. He and Butler went inside as soon as he was out of sight.

"Make a note to have a security team come in tomorrow and have things beefed up. I don't want him to be able to get back on the property again." Butler said he would. "And call Jimmy. Have him bring in some patrols for me for the next few weeks. I want to make sure he's gone."

"I will." Butler put the gun back in the wall where he'd had a gun box put in recently. "The missus, sire, is in the living room. If she sleeps there much longer, I fear she'll be sore."

"I'm taking her up now." He stood there, looking at the door to the room where she was. "I don't want to hurt her anymore."

"Of course you don't, sir. She's a wonderful woman. It'll...I believe this has been a bit much for her." Samuel looked at Butler as he continued speaking. "She will need someone to love her for who she is, not who she thinks they want her to be. I think...I'm of the opinion, sir, that telling the missus she can't do something will only make her sadder."

"You think I should let her be the chef?" Butler nodded. "And what will the staff think having their mistress cook for them?"

"They'll think they're blessed that their bellies are full and that her husband is a good enough man and one that loves his wife dearly enough to allow her to be all that she needs to be." Butler flushed. "I do believe my own missus said that if Kennedy...Mrs. Payne...wasn't able to do something, she might...she might harm herself by crawling into a shell and not returning."

From what he'd seen of her earlier, he was thinking that Butler might be right. Kennedy wasn't speaking to anyone and had stared off into space for so long that he'd run. Going into the living room, he found her curled into a tight ball with a small blanket over her. When he pulled it off her, he noticed the tears that had stained her face. Picking her up, he carried her to the bedroom, their room.

~~~

Kennedy felt the movement under her and thought of her da taking her to bed. When she realized that he was gone and she wasn't at home, she struggled to get out of the arms before she realized who had her. When Samuel spoke, she wasn't any more thrilled than she'd been when she thought that Shamus had her.

"You're going to make me drop you. Stop that." She demanded that he let her go. "I will, but not on the stairs. You were lying on the couch for a long while, and you might be a little wobbly."

"I most certainly am not." When he put her on her feet, she did nearly fall over and would have tumbled down the stairs had he not grabbed her. Before she could pull back from him, he picked her up in his arms again. "Will you put me down?"

"No." She noticed that they were in another part of the house that she'd never been in, and before she could get a good look around, she also noticed that Samuel had no shirt on. She jerked her arms from around his neck so quickly that she nearly made them both fall. He started cursing and she braced herself for the hit.

"I won't hit you. And I wish you'd believe me." He put her down on the floor again just inside the bedroom. "I may want to paddle your bottom to see it pink up, but I'd never hit you out of anger."

"And paddling my butt, that is supposed to be pleasurable?" She felt her face heat up when he looked at her. "I'm not going to have fun with you in the bed. We'll have sex when necessary but nothing else."

"Oh yes, if it's done right it can be very pleasurable. For us both. And who decides when it's necessary? You or me?" She flushed deeper and turned away from him. He was much too delicious looking without his shirt on. And her fingers itched to run through the hair on his chest. "Kennedy?"

"I don't think more than once or twice a week is necessary. You'll want a child, of course, but there is no reason that we should subject ourselves to having it for pleasure." He laughed, and she turned to him. "I'm being very serious. I've thought this out, and this is what I'd like."

"I don't think so. Maybe if you had said once or twice an hour might have been okay, but I don't think that once I'm inside of you that your arrangements are going to work. You see, I'm very sexual and will need to sate my lust on you several times a day." He moved toward her, and she took a step back. The thought of more than once a day with this man was making her think all sorts of things, and when he stopped and sniffed the air, she knew that he could smell her. "You're aroused."

She shook her head, and he grinned. "I don't know what you're talking about. I'm never...I have never had sex, so being aroused is something you're making up." He nodded and moved toward her again and backed her into the wall. "This isn't...you should just let me get on the bed. You can do whatever you want there. And the lights need to be off."

"I think we can do a great deal right here. And I plan on doing a great many things to you. With the lights on." She shook her head, but he wasn't paying attention to her. "Do you have any idea how badly I want to have you come in my mouth?"

"That's not sex. We're only going to have sex." His chuckle made her nipples harden, and when he moved to her throat, she felt her body tighten. "Mr. Payne, you have to stop this."

"I'm your husband, Kennedy. Do you think you can call me by my first name?" She shook her head again, and he licked her throat. "You taste so much better than the first time I tasted you. Like peaches. And you smell delicious too. Like a woman who is in need of her mate."

"You don't want this any more than I do." Samuel put his hands on her waist and pulled her closer to him. She tried to fight him off by pushing him away, but her fingers got tangled in his furred chest. He moaned against her ear.

"Touch me, Kennedy. Touch me like I'm going to touch you." Her fingers moved over his chest until she found his nipple. It was as hard as hers felt, and she pinched it. When he moaned, she pulled her hands away and put them behind her back. He shook his head and brought them back to him. "You should know that for as much as you touch me, I'm going to return the favor."

"Why?" Her voice was husky sounding to her ears, and she wondered what he thought of her. "You can't possibly want to have more than just sex with me. Can you? The act is just…well, I'm sure you know that it's verily messy."

"Christ, I hope so." He put his hands on her shirt and watched her eyes as he pulled it apart. When he tore it open, buttons scattering all over the room, she felt her breath catch and her heart start to pound. "You're very naïve for someone as old as you are. Didn't you ever want to fool around in the back of the car with some boy from high school?"

"I went to an all-girls school. And while some of them…played with each other, I never did. I was there to get an education, not experiment." Samuel laughed, and she jerked her shirt together. "I think I'd like to sleep in another room."

"You can do that if you want, but it won't matter much. Wherever you are, I'm going to be. But this bed is the biggest in the house, and I plan on using every inch of it with you." Her shirt was torn from her body this time. He reached for her pants; she nearly begged him to stop when they too were in pieces on the floor. Kennedy stood before him in her bra and panties, and he was looking at her like she was a meal instead of a person.

"You're looking at me like you want to eat me." She flushed when she realized what she'd said. "That's not what I meant."

Samuel dropped to his knees in front of her and pulled her forward. As much as she wanted to protest, she wanted to see what he was going to do. When he nuzzled his mouth over her mound, she tried to pull back.

"I am going to eat you. And drink from you." He looked up at her as he curled his fingers into her panties at her hips. "You're going to come for me, aren't you?"

"No, I don't think—" He tore them off her, and she tried to cover herself. But he moved her hands out of the way and opened her thighs. She let him position her the way he wanted. Her mind had shut down, and nothing on her body was listening to her anyway. As soon as he pulled her nether lips open, she felt her juices begin to trickle down her legs. Her hope was that he'd not seen it, but she knew that when he licked her that he had.

"Please, you must stop." For an answer, he suckled her clit into his mouth, and she nearly cried out. The more he ate at her the more she needed from him. And when he bit her clit again, she came hard and cried out his name.

"Again. Come again for me. I love the taste of you." She didn't think she could have stopped from coming if someone had a gun to her head. Over and over he brought her to release until she wasn't sure she could stand. But when he lifted his head from her, his mouth wet from her, she felt her body react with need, wondering how that was even possible.

Samuel stood up and kissed her. He ate at her mouth as vigorously as he had her body. And for some reason that made her needy all the more. When he pulled back from her, she whimpered and reached for him, but stopped when he started to unsnap his pants.

"You're a virgin, and as much as I hate the thought of hurting you, I'm afraid it will the first time." She glanced at the bed then at him as he leaned over to pull his jeans off. When he stood up, she took a step back. He was so large. "You'll have to trust me, I will fit."

"No, I don't think you will." Kennedy wanted to touch him to see if he felt like he looked. When he took her hand and wrapped it around him, she moaned. Rocking into her hand, she felt the skin heat beneath her touch and the soft flesh was wonderfully different than the hard steel of him.

"I want to be inside of you when I come." Nodding, she realized that she didn't care right now. The ache of wanting him made her weak in the knees. "Christ, you're beautiful."

"Nay, I'm not. But you're kind to say so." She watched as a pearly white drop appeared on the tip of his cock. She wanted to lean down and taste it and nearly did so when he jerked her head up and pulled her to him.

"I'm sorry, love, but I can't wait any longer." He lifted her up, and her feet went around him and locked at her ankles. As he took them to the bed, he lifted her high enough that her breast was at his mouth, and he bit her. Kennedy cried out and wrapped her hands into his hair, thinking to pull him away when he sucked hard on her, and she came apart again. When her back touched the bed, he wasted no time in moving her to the center still surrounding him. His cock at her entrance made her still.

"If you tense up, it's going to hurt more." Kennedy looked him in the eyes as he held her. "I need for you to bite me when we come. We'll be mated when you do. I'll bite you as well."

He slammed forward, the pain taking her breath away. Samuel didn't move for several seconds, and she felt the tears roll down her face. He told her over and over he was sorry, but she knew that this was a necessity, like all things that were going to happen from now on. When he began to move, slowly at first, she moaned. Her body was moving up to another climax, and when he licked her throat, she felt it crash over her.

She didn't bite him. Kennedy had started to twice but couldn't do it. Mates were for lovers and people who loved each other. She was a way to a means for him, and becoming his mate or not was going to be her decision. Even if it killed her.

Samuel roared against her shoulder. His teeth torn into her flesh deeply, but it didn't hurt like she'd thought it would. Something moved over her when he came inside her, triggering her own release again. She might be his wife now, but she wasn't going to be his mate. When he dropped over her, his weight felt good, but he rolled over and took her with him.

"Next time," he said to her softly. "Next time you'll bite me, and we'll be truly one."

Kennedy didn't want to be one with him. She wanted to be herself. When she felt his even breathing beneath her cheek, and his heart returned to a normal beat, she pulled away from him to find another bed. But she got no farther than an inch away when he pulled her back. He held her to him all night, and finally, exhaustion took her under.

Chapter 8

Samuel woke and reached for her again. Kennedy had been so responsive all night that he found that right now he wanted to hold her to him. Then maybe they could shower together. But all he got was cold sheets and a pillow that smelled of her. He sat up in bed and looked around.

The room was set to rights. Her clothes were gone from the floor where he'd torn them from her, and his own pants were lying over the chair near the fireplace. He didn't know where her things were, but he was pretty sure if she'd left this room, it was either wearing his things or she was naked. Either way, he wanted to find her.

Reaching out beyond the room to the rest of the house, he didn't find her there either. He was beginning to get worried when he asked his mom where Kennedy was.

She went to get her things and to go to work. I didn't know she had two jobs when I hired her, did you? He started to tell her that she dinna have any job but to be his wife when he thought of what Butler said. *She said she'd be back in time to make supper. Are you keeping her on as cook until you find someone?*

I'm not sure what we're doing. And he didn't either. *She likes to cook, and it might make her feel happy if she can. Not full-time, but for now.*

His mom agreed with him. *She made us breakfast before she left. If you hurry, you can join us. The rolls are about to come out of the oven now.*

Samuel reached for Kennedy again and felt the block she'd put up. If she'd bitten him last night, she would no longer be able to do that. But then, they had the rest of their lives to get this sorted out. He was washing his hair when he realized that he knew nothing about her. Not where she lived or worked, as a matter of fact. He decided that the two of them needed to sit down and talk. And he had to tell his mom what happened with his father.

He walked into the kitchen in time to see Butler taking what looked like fresh biscuits out of the oven and a casserole dish that smelled like heaven. He took the larger dish from him and sat it on the table. Christ, she'd made this?

"She said that I was to make sure that it cooked for one hour. I was having to keep the others from taking it out sooner. Have you ever smelled anything that good before?" Butler shook his head as he continued. "My Lord, we'll weigh a ton if she cooks for us much longer."

Right now, Samuel was having a hard time concentrating on anything but how starved he suddenly was. There were sliced tomatoes as well as gravy that had to be heated slowly so it wouldn't "break." He had no idea what that meant but pouring it over his portion made him whimper. His first bite had him moaning aloud.

There were eggs and sausage along with cubed potatoes that were browned to a nice crisp. Onions and peppers were in it as well, but in long strips so that if anyone didn't like them they could pick them out. Not one person at the table did anything with them but munch them down with the rest. The gravy was white and thick, tiny pieces of sausage mingled in with the slight garlicky taste that had him going back for seconds, then thirds. Samuel also managed to eat five of the most mouthwatering biscuits he'd ever put in his mouth.

When he put down his fork, it was because he couldn't breathe, he was so full. He looked at Butler, shocked. "Christ, were we supposed to save some for Kennedy?"

"No, My Lord, she said that she didn't eat this heavy for breakfast. She said it slows her down." Samuel realized that this was the second time he'd called him lord. He asked him about it. "We've looked up the house. The one you and Mrs. Kennedy now own. It's...shall I show you?"

When he left to get his computer, the others cleaned the table. His mother was sipping her tea when she looked up. She smiled at him, and he grinned back. He'd never felt this good in his life.

"You're falling in love with her, aren't you?" The question startled him. He started to tell her no, but she continued before she could. "Kennedy is depressed, did you know that? When she left here this morning, there were circles under her eyes. I realized that as a newly bonded couple there would be little sleep, but it didn't look like that."

"What do you mean?" Samuel decided to ignore the reference on why they had little sleep and concentrate on why she thought it was different. "By the way, do you know where she works when she leaves here or, for that matter, where she lives? I don't want her out alone so long as father is in the area."

"I don't. She never mentioned it to me other than today. She told me that she wasn't going to leave the people that had given her a place to stay in a lurch. The poor girl seemed to think you'd have a fit when you found out." Samuel shifted on his seat but said nothing. He had been upset with her at first, but he could see that she had work ethics. "The sale of the horses bothered her, did you know that?"

"Her grandmother told me that her father left them to her. She said that some of them are prized champions." His mom nodded. "But there's something else, isn't there? What do you know?"

Instead of telling him, she said something else. He felt like she'd given him the keys to something great when she suggested that he woo her. And not only that, but to make her a partner in his life and not to treat her like her father had treated her. "She's not like me, thankfully. She's got a backbone and not afraid to use it. But right now she's been overwhelmed by us all and made to do something that has taken a great deal from her. Kennedy believes you only married her for the estate."

Butler came into the room then with his wife and the laptop. Brigitte was smiling at him as she pointed to the screen. There in front of him wasn't a smallish house like he'd envisioned, but a castle, including a drawbridge.

"The original laird asked the townspeople if they'd not tell anyone that there was a castle there. He explained to them that if the neighboring lands knew of it, they'd come and rape and pillage the village in an attempt to take the castle. They all voted and decided that he was correct, and they started calling it a manor. Rose, the name of the manor, was the laird's wife. There is a large rose garden in the back with her first roses in it." Brigitte moved the cursor to the next picture. "There are orchards there as well, brimming with all sorts of fresh fruit in the summer and fall. And see here, there are the paddocks. Kennedy said that the house sits on five thousand acres including the town. Which she told us you now run too."

He was handed a packet of photos, and they all shared what each one represented. There were pictures of the trees in full bloom, as well as two with Kennedy riding the horses through the fields. Better pictures of the house and grounds too, with the grounds all neatly trimmed and cleaned in the foreground. Samuel was overwhelmed by what he was seeing.

He looked at the Internet and found out that the house had nineteen bedrooms and ten baths on the upper floor alone. There was a kitchen that could be used to serve over a thousand guests, and had several times over the years. Many times over the years the house had been home to many battles, and the house used as a makeshift hospital. It told how Kennedy's father, the Earl of Lambton, had brought the house from near ruin forty years ago and also made the town prosperous.

"She lived there." His mom nodded at him. "I thought that she needed me to care for her, to make her...I don't know...have things I could provide for her. But she...she has all this."

"No, Samuel, you both do if you'll allow her." He looked at the pictures and then back at his mom. "You're overwhelmed."

"No shit." She laughed at him, and so did Brigitte. "I'm sorry, but...how does this make me a lord? This is her family. I'm just...just a guy from Illinois." He looked up when a small laugh caught his attention. Dani came to him as she entered the room.

"The title came with your marriage to my granddaughter. And as soon as Shamus is disinherited, you'll take the title of Lord Lambton as well." Dani kissed his cheek. "Hello, dear.

How are you today? Looking up your family history, I see. Would you like to discuss the money now?"

"How much...? Christ I know this sounds greedy, but how much money are we talking here? I know that you said that with the marriage came her money, but I thought that she wasn't...." Samuel took a deep breath, trying to gather his questions. "You said she wouldn't receive anything because she was a daughter. I don't have the kind of money to keep a house like this."

"Kennedy is from a long and very prosperous line. Her grandmothers have been providing for her as the first daughter for all their generations. As Kennedy will for her own daughter. Over the years, decades really, the women realized that as first daughter she'd be the one that would be married off for more money. Titled money as it were. They dinna like it any more than Kennedy does now. They provided her with a means to say no. Gave her enough money that she could simply do as she damned well please and tell her family to screw off." She thanked Butler for the tea he set in front of her as she continued. "Over the ensuing years only one of the descendants used it, and she ended up finding her own love years later and paid the money back. I've never been more happy for that time in all my life."

Samuel smiled. "It was why you helped Kennedy escape and get her education. You wanted her to be free of her family long before...hell, a very long time before her dad died."

"I did. I could see that she needed more. Much more than the milksops there could give her. I never thought she'd meet a man such as yourself, but then it was only recently that I had an idea what you were. Kennedy had her first encounter with her boss and his mate. The Savages I believe their names were." She handed him a rolled up parchment, and he held it gently in his hands as she explained. "It's the deed to the house, as well proof that all back monies have been paid off. And in answer to your question, the estate isn't indebted at all now, so it's worth is just over one hundred million American dollars. Of course, that doesn't include the furnishings and cars. My husband was quite the collector, and those are being returned to the garage as we speak. I had them removed before my son died."

Samuel didn't open the envelope she handed him either. He needed to see Kennedy. Now he understood so much more about his wife that he never did before. He wanted to tell her how sorry he was; no, he wanted to beg her to forgive him. He'd treated her no differently than generations back had treated their own mates.

"Where is she, do you know?" Dani nodded. "I don't expect for her to forgive me, but I do need to ask her. She deserves so much more than I've done to her."

"And you care why? You have the house, young man. The estate is yours now that you've bedded her. What reason could you have to ask her to forgive you now?" He saw the gleam in her eyes and understood the question.

"Because I need her to complete me. I need Kennedy because she's all I've ever needed in a wife and mate, and I was too stupid to realize it." He looked at the computer screen that had gone dark. "If this means giving up all of this so she'll believe me, then I will. I want her to trust me, because right now she doesn't trust anyone."

Dani nodded at him and stood up. She handed him another piece of paper, and on this one was an address. "She's there working. It was to provide her with an address so she could buy her own home. She wanted something to call her own. I don't think she's ever had anything of her own until now."

Samuel took the paper and moved out to the garage. He looked at the address for the first time and laughed. She lived in Savage Campground. And a savage was coming to get her. Laughing hard for the first time in weeks, Samuel climbed into his big SUV and went after his own little savage. Time to tame the beasts in her.

~~~

Kennedy was walking the perimeter again just because she could when she realized she was being watched. The hair danced on her neck and arms, but she kept going in the same direction. She had her bat with her, but she was afraid that it was going to do her little good. When something growled behind her, she turned slowly to see the biggest fucking lion she'd ever seen.

"Nice kitty." He growled again as he made his way toward her. When she lifted the bat up, thinking that maybe she might be able to hit him once before he tore her apart, he stopped moving. "I don't think you're Samuel, are you?"

The big lion shook his head and roared at her. Even as far as the ten feet he was away from her, she could feel the heat of his breath. And the size of his teeth made her think that when he did bite her, he was going to be able to chomp her in half with one bite of those powerful jaws. Mother fuck, he was going to kill her.

Fear tore through her, and she wanted to turn and run from him. But she knew that he wanted her to run. She'd read somewhere that lions, like all predators, liked to chase down their meals. Swallowing hard, she thought of Samuel and wondered what he'd do when he found her, if he found her.

Kennedy? Her body wanted to sag in relief when he spoke to her. *What's wrong? I can feel your terror. Where are you?*

Aye, I am in terror. It's running through my veins like whiskey in an Irishman. A big fucking cat is standing in front of me, and he looks hungry. I doona wanna die this way. I thought he were you. Then I asked him and he said he wasn't. Then when he…I'm going to die, aren't I? She was babbling, and she knew it. But the fact that she could speak at all made her feel like she wasn't completely losing it. *I doona wanna be eaten alive by this mon.*

You won't. Just stay calm and don't run. She told him she wasn't sure her feet would allow her to anyway. *That's my girl. I'm on my way there now. I'm about ten minutes out.*

I doona think he's gonna wait for you to come rescue me. He's coming closer now. She watched as he took small steps until he was only about five feet from her. *Aye, he's gonna kill me. You should be glad that you doona see this. Is mian liom raibh mé in ann a fhoghlaim chun grá agat mar ba chóir dom a dhéanamh.* Wishing she really had been able to love him like a wife did a man was all she had left to tell him as the lion leapt at her.

She brought the bat up as he hit her with his body. She knew it connected with something the way it jarred her arms. He let her go, but she was bleeding pretty badly and knew that if she gave up now, she might as well let him have her. As soon as she got her feet under her again, she brought the bat up again and hit him with it in the front arm. He roared at her and snapped at her again. When his teeth sank into her thigh, she brought the bat down over and over onto his head until he let her go. Dropping to the ground, she nearly let the darkness take her when he was suddenly over her.

The bat was slick in her hands. She couldn't see what it was but thought it was hers and his blood. Lifting it took a great deal of effort, but she brought it around hoping to connect with his mouth and hit him in the leg, the other one this time. He went tumbling over her and lay still. Before he could get up and have at her again, Kennedy knew that if she didn't kill him now that he'd kill her.

She must have blacked out once but knew that it could only have been for a few seconds. The lion lay still, but she could see that he was still breathing. It was labored like hers, but he would still likely kill her if he got up. Trying to sit up to do what she needed she nearly passed out when she got a look at her body. He'd really hurt her.

Her legs were torn to ribbons. Long lines of open flesh bled onto the fresh snow. Her pants, her only pair, were stained with it so much that they were dark with blood. She had a sudden thought that she'd never get them clean no matter how many times she washed them. One boot was missing, but her foot was still attached to her ankle, which she found she was profoundly grateful for.

Her left arm hurt so badly that she knew it had to be broken. She tried to move her fingers, and she nearly threw up on herself when she realized that one of his teeth was still in her skin. One of her fingers was nearly bitten off and hung on by the merest of skin. She looked around for her watch, a gift from her da when she'd turned sixteen, and found it shattered near the big beast. Tears stung her eyes, and she cried out when the salty mixture touched a wound on her face. Reaching up with her good hand she cried out again when she realized that her lip was torn open and her nose was split as well.

If she didn't get help within the next few minutes she was going to bleed to death. She looked at the blood surrounding her and figured that if a team of medics were there now, they more than likely couldn't save her. The lion stirred slightly, and she decided that she had to get up or be his next meal.

Samuel told her he was almost there. *'Tis too late for us both. We're already dead. I'm so sorry, Samuel. Tell Seanmháthair that I love her.*

Kennedy stood up, only to stumble twice. Using the bat as a crutch, she moved to where the big lion lay and put the cracked thing over her shoulder. Do or die time, she thought. When he turned to her and roared again, his paw scraped her belly, and she stabbed the bat down his throat. It was all she could manage before she fell to the ground again. Closing her eyes, she thought she heard her name but was too far gone to hold on. Suddenly, Samuel was there.

Is breá liom tú. She tried to lift her arm to touch him, but it was too difficult. She told him once again that she loved him.

She opened her eyes when he screamed at her. Kennedy was suddenly very cold and told him so. She had no idea if he understood her or not, but suddenly she was being covered up. Every time he moved her, she cried out, but the harder she tried not to the more it seemed to hurt.

"Know him?" She hoped that he didn't, but he said he did. "Dead? I had to hurt him. He was...." She closed her eyes again only to have him tell her to open them.

"He's dead. And even if you hadn't killed him, he would have died anyway for hurting you. Stay with me, baby. Please? Help is on the way." She watched his mouth move but was having a hard time understanding what he might be talking about. "I can't change you without help. Just stay with me until he gets here."

"I'm hurt," she said. He sobbed then and told her he knew. "Tired. I'm tired." Closing her eyes was hard when he kept telling her to stay with him. When she saw someone else there, she didn't understand why the man from the house would come to see her. But asking was no longer an option.

She screamed when she felt someone bite her again. This time she couldn't have stopped the darkness from taking her if he begged her not to.

The last sound she heard was screaming. It took her several seconds just before she went under to realize it was her. Christ. She was screaming like a little girl.

Chapter 9

From the moment that he'd landed in this forsaken country, he'd been cold. How these people lived like this was beyond him. If Shamus didn't need to complete this mission, he'd take his ticket and turn it in for a sooner flight. But as it was now, he'd either find Kennedy or it would be the end of him.

The phone call he'd gotten as soon as he was off the plane had frightened him somewhat. Donald was screaming into the phone for him to come back now. When a voice, very calm and self-assured, took over the call, Shamus felt his bladder nearly loosen. His agent was not a happy man.

"Those horses you sold me were taken back yesterday. You said you had the papers on them to sell. And since I've no bill of lading I'm being investigated along with you. I have a great deal to hide, Shamus Buehler, to have the coppers looking into me and mine." Alton Stockberry was not a man to trifle with. Shamus should have known better.

"They're me sisters. She's ill, as I said." He cleared his throat twice before he could continue. "Aye, that's it, she's very ill, and I needed the funds to come to her."

"So you said. But what I found out is that you've sold your sister off to the highest bidder and she ran. Both of them. And now that you've a deadline to meet, you've decided to go and drag her back." Alton laughed. "You think that's going to work for you?"

"She'll listen to me or else feel the back of me hand again." Shamus hated looking stupid, and his sisters had made him look a fool. "I'll get yer monies back to you as soon as I get her."

"I don't want the money now. I want Kennedy." The back of his neck seemed to dance with live wires. Shamus started to tell him that she was promised to another when Alton laughed again. "And you'll bring her to me. I don't care if you have to beat her to do so."

"Aye, but…well, I owe her to someone else. He's taking her for another debt I owe." Shamus watched the people come and go around him, and he wondered if he could simply take one of them back with him and pawn her off as his sister. "You ever meet my sisters?"

"I've seen both of them in photographs. So don't be thinking you can pull a switch on me. I'll know her." So much for that plan, he thought. "I'm coming there now. I've chartered a plane and should be there by five your time. What part of that little part of Ireland are you in anyway?"

He'd thought he was still home. Shamus had been so glad that he'd not told anyone where he was going, especially not his friend Donald. After he'd given him directions to Rose Manor, Shamus had gotten off the phone quickly. He had no idea if the man was tracing the call or not, but he suddenly dinna trust him. Now here he was standing in front of a hotel counter where his family was staying.

"I dinna care that you have policies. I have me own polices. It's to talk to me family." The woman looked like she might hit him, but Shamus was prepared for that. If she did, he'd own her and this building. "Get them to me now."

"I've said this several times now, and I refuse to say it again. So I want you to listen up asshole. For the ninth time. I will not under any circumstances bring you anyone from this hotel even if it meant you were going to live for another five seconds and I'd have the opportunity to piss on your head." He was taken aback by her rudeness, but before he could say anything else, he was grabbed from behind. "Take this piece of shit out of here and toss his miserable ass out into the streets."

And the two men who held him did just that. He was picking himself up from the snow when his phone rang. Pulling it out, he nearly snarled into the receiver when he realized who it was on the other end. His grandmother's caller ID flashed with her picture. And she would not like it snarling at her, he thought with a laugh.

"Hello, Shamus. My name is Samuel Payne, and you may not know it yet, but I'm going to kick your ass all over this state before this is finished. By the way, did you get snow in your knickers when you were tossed out on your arse?" The laugher that came over the line made him look around. He was afraid the man was too close and would carry out his threat.

"Where are you? If you have my grandmother's phone, you must know where they are?" Shamus looked around again and wondered again where the mon was. "You'll tell me this minute because I have urgent business with them."

"You mean selling off your sister to get your ass out of trouble? Not going to happen. I've already married her. Kennedy and I are starting our life together, and you're not welcome in it." Shamus felt his knees weaken, and he fell into the snow again. The man had to be lying.

"You canna marry my sister without my permission. I'm her guardian, and she canna marry anyone unless I say she can." It was almost true what he'd told Samuel. Kennedy was his sister. "If you've bedded her, then there will be consequences for your actions."

"I'm thinking that you're up the creek without a paddle then." Shamus had no idea what that meant, but it mattered little. If he really had married Kennedy, then he was the heir to the estate. That made him laugh.

"You think to marry my sister for her money? 'Tis gone. All of it. Nary a copper to her name and even her horses, those precious bags of bones father left her, are gone." Shamus stood up suddenly, feeling as if he'd gotten one over the mon. "Kennedy is worthless to you. Bring her to me and I'll give you whatever you want."

"I have what I want." The words were spoken with a harshness that made Shamus think that he'd rather have Alton looking for him than this man. "As for Rose Manor, I've taken measures to ensure its well-being. Right now it's secured with people who will care for it until my wife and I can visit. Even the title has been given to me. I'm the new Earl of Lambton."

"You lie." That title was his no matter what his financial situation was. "You canna take my title from me. By birth it's given to the first son. I worked hard in making sure it went to me."

"How hard did you work?" The question was asked softly, and it was on the tip of his tongue to tell the mon just how hard it had been to kill his own da. How difficult it was to make sure that none of the others were given their due when he died by forging the will that left him nothing and everything to Kennedy. He almost told him that he had had to practice for days on end before killing him to ensure he looked like the grieving son, that he had put camphor into his kerchief to cause the tears to flow.

"I'll see you in hell before I let you take my birthright." The mon laughed again, and Shamus was sure this time that he'd heard him near and not just on the phone. "Where are you? Where did you take my family?"

"Look to your right." Shamus turned only to hear the man laugh again. "Your other right, you moron. Don't they teach you your left from right in How to be a Villain school?"

Again the reference eluded him but Shamus turned to look. He stumbled back when he saw the wolf standing there. When he lifted his paw and waved at him, Shamus took a step back and walked into someone. The arm that wrapped around his throat had him wet his pants.

"Don't move." The man's voice was the one from the phone. "I could snap your neck right now and no one would care other than that you blocked the sidewalk."

"You're hurting me." The man laughed, and Shamus felt his breath fan across his cheek. "Please doona hurt me."

"You'll stay away from my family. If you don't, that big wolf over there and I are going to hunt you down and tear you to pieces. Then we'll bury you in a shallow grave so that any hungry animal that comes along can feast on your bones." A hard shake had his teeth rattle together. "Do you understand me?"

"Aye, I do. Just give me Kennedy back and we'll call it—" His arm was brought behind him quickly, and Shamus screamed when he felt it snap. "You've broken my arm."

"That's not all I'll break if you come near my wife again." He was suddenly shoved forward and hit his face on the car parked at the curb. Blood seemed to erupt from his nose and mouth, but before he could turn and ask the man again to just give him Kennedy, the mon was gone. And so was the wolf.

Shamus cradled his arm in his hand and moved toward the hotel again. The two men from earlier were standing there and wouldn't allow him to come in. He asked them for medics to aide him when one of them said that the police had been called. Shamus sat in the snow and waited. As the snow started to melt into his pants, he thought that he'd be able to hide the fact that he'd pissed himself. Fucking bastard was going to pay for that.

~~~

Kennedy opened her eyes slowly. She was afraid that the lion was still alive, and when he found her awake, he was going to finish the job. When the light proved to be too much for her, she closed her eyes again and waited. The small laugh had her looking to her right.

"You're awake finally." Kennedy nodded at Summer. "I've been a little concerned, but the doctor said you'd be fine now. He attributed you being out for so long to the loss of blood. I thought it was because you were simply exhausted. Either way, you're awake now."

"Hurt." Summer nodded to her and reached for her hand. "Hurt badly." She did too. Not as bad as she'd thought she would but... Summer had said something about a doctor and looked at her. "Lion?"

"Yes, there was a lion there. The news is saying that he must have escaped from the zoo. Of course the zoo is denying such a thing happened, but there was a lion there." She smiled, and Kennedy felt a little dizzy. "You'll need to rest more darling. As soon as Samuel returns, he'll explain to you what happened."

"The lion? He's dead?" Summer nodded again. "Not Samuel, but he said he knew him somehow."

"Yes, he was his father. You killed his father." Summer moved to the door, the whine of the chair loud in the room. "I would thank you for that, but I'm afraid that you'll think horribly of me."

With that she moved out of the door, and as it closed behind her, Kennedy wondered why she wasn't in jail, and realized that in order to put her in jail she'd have to be healthy enough to be there. That made her laugh a little, and when the door opened again, she expected to see men in strait jackets, or at the very least handcuffs. Samuel standing there made her blink several times.

"Mom said you were awake. I'm so glad. I was terrified I'd been too late." She looked away from him, trying to remember what had happened. She remembered the lion that attacked her and that she'd killed him, but the rest was sort of fuzzy. She turned back to him when he whispered her name.

"When do they take me away?" He frowned at her. "For murder. I can't tell you I'm sorry that I killed your dad, but he was bent on killing me."

"The police are saying you're one very lucky woman. Rarely does a person live from the kinds of wounds you sustained." He leaned forward as he brought her hand to his mouth and kissed it. "If I had been one minute later, you would have been dead. One minute."

She looked away from him. Kennedy wondered why he didn't just wait the one minute and let her die. When he said her name again, she turned to look at him, and he smiled at her. She wasn't sure what to make from that look.

"You have to know what I did. I had no choice. I'm sorry that I couldn't ask you or even explain to you what we did, but there wasn't time." Samuel started pacing, and she watched him as he continued. "I'd called Jimmy to come and help me kill my father. He's a wolf and would have been able to help me track him. But when I got there, you'd already…you'd taken care of him."

"He attacked me. I dinna do anything to him. Suddenly he was just there behind me. When I was speaking to you, I knew that he was going to kill me." Kennedy looked down at her body, expecting to see tubes and padding. Blood had been all over her, and now she was…. Kennedy threw back the covers and looked at her legs. They were healed, as well as her arms. Lifting her gown up, she pressed her hand over her smooth belly and looked at Samuel.

"I changed you," he said. She nodded, then shook her head. "Into a lioness. If I hadn't, then you would have died, and I didn't want that. Couldn't want that. I need you."

"How did you…?" She tried to think, and she remembered the pain. "You bit me. You had Mr. Burger hold me down and you bit me."

"Even as weak as you were, you were still strong enough to throw Jimmy off. I…I had to start before he got to us, and you'd already hit me several times before he could hold you for me. But the conversion took a great deal out of you. The loss of blood made your change slow, and you still nearly died. By the time the police showed up, I had finished, but…. You still might have died."

She laid her head back on the pillow. "Why do the police think that a lion attacked me? Wouldn't he have changed when he died? Changed back I mean?"

"The bat you used was silver, or at least had some in the coating. And when you…Christ, I have no idea how you did that as wounded as you were, but when you shoved it down his gullet, the silver, even though there is very little in the bat, was enough to keep him as a lion until he was completely dead. When we shift back as we're dying it happens at the moment we take our last breaths. He couldn't because of the way you killed him."

"Murdered him." Samuel shook his head. "He might have been attacking me at the time, but I murdered him."

"He contacted me just before he attacked you. Father told me that he could smell me on you. Knew that we were mates and that he was going to enjoy killing you." Samuel came back to the bed and pulled her into his arms. "He was going to kill you because he thought to make me suffer. He said it was for all the things I'd done to him, and he wanted me to pay with blood. I don't think he expected my little Irish Rose to fight back, and certainly didn't expect you to be able to kill like you did."

She enjoyed him holding her, and when she leaned into his chest, she felt something move along her skin and pulled back from him. He was looking at her with the strangest look on his face.

"It's your lioness. She wants my lion." Kennedy pulled back from him more, but he pulled her back. "Nuzzle into my neck and see if that calms her."

As soon as she smelled him, she wanted him. It was as if a switch had been turned on and she was suddenly needy. Kennedy licked his throat and felt him growl low, and she pulled him closer to her. Christ, she wanted him right now.

"I can smell you. You smell like sex." Kennedy felt the purr of her cat race over her body and then spill from her lips. Samuel laid her back on the bed and took her mouth. Hunger took her, and she wanted him. When he moved over her body, climbing into the bed with her, she reached for the zipper on his pants. The sooner he was inside of her the better.

Samuel tore at her clothes. The gown was opened at her shoulder, and as soon as his mouth covered her breast, she wrapped her hand around his freed cock. Sheets were ripped when they ended up tangled around them. Buttons were torn from holes that ripped rather than came free. Samuel picked her up, and before she touched the wall behind her, his cock was buried deep within her.

"Hurry. Make me come." He growled, and she growled back. Christ, if she dinna taste him soon, she was going to explode. "I want to…. Please, I need to bite you. I don't know if I can. Help me."

He pounded into her as he licked her shoulder. When she did the same to his, he lifted his head, his eyes dark, and his face slightly furred.

"Come and bite me." His voice was harsh, almost sounding inhuman. "Let your cat go enough to bite me and come."

Samuel threw back his head and roared. Christ, he was beautiful, and when he leaned forward and sank his teeth into her shoulder, she felt her own cat rise up with the need to claim him. As soon as she bit him, Samuel roared against her wound as her climax seemed to tear her apart.

It wasn't enough. Even as she came down, her body trembling with her release, she wanted more. Wanted all of him, and when he took her to the bed and told her to turn around, she leaned into the bed and let him take her hard from behind. His cock filled her differently this time, and when he pressed her head to the bed and held her down, she felt her cat roar, and Kennedy tried to get free. But Samuel leaned over her and bit deep into her shoulder again and held her there while he fucked her.

"Mine." She heard what he said, but neither her cat nor her agreed. "You're mine now and forever. Mine, Kennedy, say it."

"Nay, I belong to no one." He reached around her and slid his finger into her aching pussy. Every time he slid past her clit she wanted to hurt him. Begging him to finish her only made him bite her harder.

"Say it and I'll give you relief. Say you belong to me and I'll give it all to you." She growled again. "You want to come? Then say it. Tell me you belong to me."

He touched her clit, a small brush of his fingers over her, and she arched up. He held her down while he took her harder, the bed moving across the floor as he did so. When he touched her again, another brief touch, she screamed out her answer, and he pinched her hard.

Her body seemed to pause for the briefest of seconds. She felt, in that moment, that she was poised on a great cliff and would fall at any moment. When Samuel tore at her shoulder, pain ripped into her, but it was just enough to throw her over the edge. Her release seemed to not just shatter her but put her back together and break her apart several times before she finished. Her mind snapped into Samuel's, and she saw his life as it flashed before her eyes. Birth to childhood, when he learned to walk. His mother holding him in the water to show him how to swim. His father hitting him for the first time, the anguish he felt when he couldn't protect his mother. Samuel's heartbreak when the doctors told him she'd never walk again. His terror at finding her in a pool of her blood, and his joy at hearing her heart beating strongly after he'd bitten her.

Blackness chased her over the edge, and when it caught her, gave her the darkness she needed when her body was lax. Kennedy heard Samuel whisper to her, and she knew he told her the truth. *"Is breá liom tú ró."*

Chapter 10

Samuel held her to him. He knew that sooner or later he'd have to tell her everything he'd done, but for now she was sated and still. Rubbing his fingers up and down her back, he touched several scars there but didn't mind them as much as he might have. Having her here, alive and well, was all that he cared about right now.

"Won't the police be suspicious when they see that I'm not hurt?" His fingers paused at her question. "I mean, they were called in, right?"

"Yes. Jimmy called them just after we knew your conversion was well on its way. You were still very hurt by the time they arrived." She lifted her head and rested it on his chest. Samuel didn't want to talk about her being hurt, but even messy and looking like she'd just been thoroughly fucked, she looked like she would hurt him. If only a little.

"You said that you changed me, and that because of the extent of the injuries, I was in bad shape when they arrived. I get that. What I doona...don't understand is what now." She pinched his nipple when he grinned at her.

"Doona hide your Irish, girl. I love it." She lifted a brow that told him she wasn't fooled for a moment. "You're dead. We...when you changed your heart rate and breathing had nearly stopped. Only another super would have been able to hear or detect it. There was a wolf with the first responders, and Jimmy told him what had happened. You were taken away by ambulance and routed here instead of the hospital where you were headed."

"I see." She laid her head back on his chest, and he felt the first tear on his chest. Lifting her up, he looked into her eyes and then pulled her to his mouth for a kiss.

"Not you, love, just...Jimmy said he'd never seen you before. He made the police believe that you were a transient. A homeless person. The damage...you wouldn't have had any prints that they could find. You're not in the system." She stared at him for long moments.

"Made the police believe it how?" Christ, she was much sharper than he needed her to be right now. Samuel hoped that his friend would forgive him for telling her his secret, but he knew that if he didn't, she'd never let it go.

"All supernaturals have one or two things they can do that set them apart from someone else. Not to say that another can do what they do, but it will be slightly different for each shifter. Jimmy can manipulate minds. It takes a great deal out of him if it's a lot of people, but he can do it." She asked him what his was. "I can speak to all species."

He waited for her to say something else, but she laid her head back down in his chest. After several minutes, he closed his eyes and started to drift to sleep. When she spoke again, it didn't startle him, but it did make his heart tighten in his chest.

"I'm mated and bonded to a were-lion. I, myself, am no longer human, and I've lost Kennedy Buehler. Now I'll be expected to do your bidding at all times and not do what I wish." She looked up at him, sadness in her eyes. "I've given it to you willingly, make no mistake, but I do wish right now that I had not."

He pulled her over him and rolled her to her back. He pulled her arms up above her head and held them there as he looked deep into her eyes. Samuel could see her fear there as well as her sorrow. While he knew that he could do nothing about what had happened to her with her being no longer human, he could show her what she gained rather than lost.

"When I came upon you at the scene, you were just dropping to the ground. My father was struggling to pull free from the bat, but he was weak from all the damage you'd done to him. I went to you to see that you'd been hurt more than I'd first thought. More than…more than any human would have been able to endure. But you still lived." He ran his hands down her arms to her heart. "I could hear your heart beating. Slow and getting slower, it seemed to call to me. And I knew in that moment that I didn't…no, I *couldn't* live without you in my life. I needed you."

"Because I'm your other half." He shook his head. "Then what?" she asked. "Because of some sense of duty? Some strange need to make sure that I did as you told me?"

"No. I needed you in my life because I love you." She looked at him, and he felt her heart beat a little faster beneath his fingers. "When you were dying in my arms, all I could think about was how badly I'd treated you. How many times I'd tossed you away."

"You aren't going to get any arguments from me." He laughed at her, and she smiled. "I wasn't any nicer to you either. Of course, I was provoked most of the time. You were trying very hard to keep me away."

"I was. Now I want only for you to be as close to me as I can get you." He rocked into her softness and watched her eyes darken with need. "Then you told me you loved me."

Kennedy turned her head away, and for a moment, he let her. When she looked back at him, he could see that she was going to try to blow it off. Before she spoke, he leaned down and took her mouth gently before looking at her again.

"I remember saying it. I thought I was dying, and…and I realized the truth of it. You've no need to repeat the words to me. I've no desire to—"

"I do. Have a desire, as well as a need, to love you." Samuel grinned. "It took me two days to try and figure out what you'd said to me, and another two to learn how to say it back to you. Christ, that's a hard language to speak."

"Cad a bheadh sé a ghlacadh chun tú a stoptar suas agus a mbíonn gnéas acu le orm arís?" He made out three of the words before he got the general meaning. Samuel cupped her breast into his hand and thumbed her nipple until it was hard.

"I can shut up and make love to you, but there will be no more sex between us." He rocked into her again and was pleased to see her eyes flutter closed. "Kennedy, we're going to make love from now on. It may be rough and hard. I may take you against a tree or a wall, but it will be forever making love."

He leaned down and pulled her pert nipple into his mouth and nipped. She arched up off the bed for him, and he opened his mouth wider over the tasty morsel and sucked hard enough to bring a moan from her. Samuel rolled to his back and adjusted her over his cock. He smiled when she rode his cock, then moaned when she lifted herself up and held him while lowering herself onto his cock.

"Kennedy. Christ, woman, ride me." He moved her hips back and forth to give her an idea what he wanted. Then he held on to keep from flying away. Samuel wasn't sure who was teaching who when she threw back her head and rolled her breasts in her hands.

Nothing could have prepared him for the beauty of her. Her body was slim and lean, her face a study in concentration. Pinked nipples begged to be suckled. Her skin had a fine sheen of sweat as her fingers moved down her body to her pussy. Samuel sat up and pulled her body closer, wishing he were at home so he could take her properly on their big bed.

"Come for me," he said. She moaned and wrapped her fingers into his hair. "Come for me, Kennedy, so I can fill you."

She bowed back and grabbed his shoulders. When she dug her nails deep into him, he watched as she came. As it moved up her body and a scream spilled from her mouth. Samuel was so mesmerized by her that when his own release took him he cried out too and took her throat hard.

Blood filled his mouth. It was hot, spicy, and made his cock jerk again inside of her. When she licked his shoulder, he moved her to her back and pounded deep as she sank her own teeth into him. Samuel thought he was prepared for her bite, but when her teeth tore at his skin, he felt as if the world centered for him. His body and mind were now not just his but hers as well. Everything came to a single thought—Kennedy Payne was his.

Stars burst behind his eyelids; his body tensed more for another climax that took his breath away. Lifting his head up, he roared out, the sound of it echoing around the room as she fell back to the bed, her eyes closed, her body lax. Samuel dropped atop her, not even having enough energy to move off her in the event he was too heavy. Closing his eyes, he thought only to rest for a second, but sleep claimed him.

Never had he felt like this with a woman before and knew deep in his heart, he never would again.

~~~

"Yer looking for anybody in particular up there?" Alton sat on the chair that was a good deal softer than the car seat he'd rented to get this far. He looked at the man standing next to him and tried to get up the energy to be pissed he was dripping beer condensation on his suit.

"I was looking for the oldest, Shamus, but if any of the others are here, that would be fine as well." The man nodded, then simply sat down. When a draft was set in front of both men, the man put his beefy hand into the handle of one while he finished off the one he'd brought.

"They be gone. About...." He looked at the bartender. "How long you guess there that the Rose Manor has been empty?"

"Seachtain nó dhó." Alton looked at his companion and was told a week or two. Then when the bartender said something else, the man nodded and looked at Alton.

"Says the house has been empty of all souls for a week or two, but the missus of the house and her brood have been gone a month. Or there abouts. So ye be looking for Shamus? He's more'n likely up to no good. Boy hasn't been a lick of good since his daddy passed, God rest his soul."

Alton was confused by the exchange of conversations as well as the languages. There had to be something more than just English and Gaelic going on here. And his body ached. He wanted a hot shower, a soft bed, and three or four days of uninterrupted sleep. He doubted that he'd get any of that in his God-forsaken country. If he managed to miss a single rut or bump in the road, he'd buy the country and have each one paved. But it was the lack of fencing that had him so exhausted. The things would simply come out of nowhere to step right in front of him. Christ and heaven forbid he nearly hit one. The farmer that had berated him for nearly twenty minutes had threatened him with every tool he'd had on him. And Alton still wasn't sure that he'd been cursed too.

"Do you have any idea where he might have gone?" The man nodded and drank down his beer…he supposed it was ale not beer. When the man didn't answer him, Alton was tempted to get out his gun and blow the lot of their heads off. "Can you tell me where he and his family have gone?"

"Not the missus. She left without a word to anyone. Not even my own *bhean chéile*, wife, I mean. Said that morning that her services woulda be needed until she returned. Paid her up, she did, always did like the missus up there. She ain't got a *pingin* on the *dowager*, but then she was a mite different anyways. Her granddaughter was aliken her. Not in beauty, mind you, but…." He stopped talking and frowned. "Where was I?"

Alton didn't have a clue. He was still stuck on what a *pingin* or a *dowager* was. He knew that the latter was a title, but nothing more. When the man started talking again, Alton decided that he needed something stronger than ale, but apparently that wasn't going to happen either. Suddenly, he started paying attention when he heard Shamus mentioned.

"…to the States too, but Miss Kennedy dinna go with him. They dinna like each other. He wanting her to marry up with Tailor was all it took for her to say she'd had enough. 'Course he done beat her to near death first, but that didn't set well with the *dowager*. She near had a fit. Had me take her to the ship when there was nothing to her but a bottle of medicine feeding her poor body." Alton lifted his hand. His head was splitting and if he had to hear much more of any story he wasn't going to be responsible for what he did.

"Where is Shamus?" Nodding, the man said he was in the United States of the Americas. "Do you know where in the States?"

"Ohio." He'd said it like it was more than the few syllables than it was. Alton was barely holding onto his temper when the man started to say more. But this was much more helpful than anything else he'd been going on about. "He sold off her horses without having the proper papers. She's going to pull up her Irish when she finds him."

"Not if I find him first." The man frowned deeper. "Kennedy and her family are in Ohio too then?"

"I would say yer right. Doona know for sure, but I'd say so. Shamus got himself into some powerful trouble a few weeks back, and now he's looking for some cash. Doona know if he's found it yet, but the horses weren't his to sell." Alton stood up and had to work hard at not pulling his gun. When the bartender said something, the man looked at him and winked. "Yer paying up for the brew? I worked up a mighty thirst."

Alton pulled out several bills and threw them on the table. He made sure that the man at his table could see the gun he'd picked up only today. As he left the door, the man whistled, and Alton looked back.

"Shamus has more'n you looking for him. Yer competitor paid me good for what he got. Too bad for you." The man stood up and laid a gun on the table beside him. "Ye harm anyone but Shamus and I'll hunt you down. We take care of what we need to."

Alton backed out of the pub. He hadn't realized that there were so many people in the place when he'd been inside, but now he could see that he should have been watching. The fifty or so people in the place stared at him as he moved out, and every one of them was armed. He was nearly to his car when the door opened and several of the patrons spilled out to watch him.

Alton started up the road again but was blocked by three of the biggest men he'd ever seen. Blazing red hair and big bodies simply stood in the street until he backed up and turned around. He was perhaps a mile down the road when he noticed that while they didn't follow him down the road, they did watch him. Alton decided that it was his first and last trip to the Emerald Isle.

Picking up his phone, he had to pull over until he had a signal. When he had what he hoped was enough to make a call, he dialed Shamus's number. It went to voicemail almost immediately. Alton thought that if Shamus had his calls set up so that they went straight to voicemail, he was going to kill the man much more slowly than he'd first thought. On the third try over three hours later, he finally got a hold of the prick.

"You lied to me." There was enough noise in the background that Alton wondered if the was at a party, and that pissed him off more. "Do you think you have something to celebrate, you motherfucker? I'm coming for you now, and you'll not be laughing it up then."

"Laughing? Are ye fucking nuts?" Then when he didn't answer, Shamus started stammering around. "I doona know what ye be talking about. I dinna lie to ye."

"Are you or are you not in the United States when I'm sitting over here in Ireland looking for your ass?" Nothing forthcoming again. "I asked you where you were. You said you'd be waiting for me to get here. What the—?"

"You dinna expect me to wait until ye got there for ye to kill me, did ye?" Laughter was not something that Alton wanted to hear from the man. "I doona know how you do things where yer from, but a mon does not wait for his death. An Irishman goes out with gusto."

Alton felt his temper snap. He'd had enough of this man and what he'd been putting up with. As soon as he thought he could speak without spewing things that wouldn't make sense to either of them, Alton spoke quietly and enunciated each word.

"When I find you, I'm going to tie you to a chair before I start cutting parts off you one at a time. I'm going to start with that tiny dick of yours and shove it up your ass. Then I'm going to take out your lying tongue." He looked around himself and felt his temper go nuclear. He'd just threatened the man with witnesses.

Closing his phone, he tried to smile off to the people surrounding him that he'd been joking. The airport was busy for this time of night, and he had to finally get up and move to another part of the lobby before he felt he could feel like a thousand eyes weren't staring at him. Alton never lost his temper, and when he did find Shamus Buehler, he was going to make him pay for that as well.

It took him over nineteen hours to get to Ohio. The plane he'd been about to board had had undiscovered issues just as they were boarding, and they had to wait on some fucking idiot to make a decision to get another plane. He had a car waiting for him in Columbus, Ohio, and simply took a hotel. He'd go the rest of the way in the morning. He was too fucking tired to mess with Shamus tonight. He called his man to see if Shamus had bolted again.

"Nah, he's holed up in some little hotel in that town I told you about earlier." Anderson was his go-to guy when Alton needed someone found and the first person he called when he wanted Shamus found. "I think he believes he's untouchable. You'd think the prick was on vacation or something?"

"He's going to be when I'm finished with him." Alton felt himself loosen up just knowing that this was nearing an end. "Have you located Kennedy yet?"

"Yeah, she's around where he is. I found an addy for you, but you're not going to be able to just go in. The guy has her in lockdown so tight that the only reason I know she's there is because I happened to see her going in. Guy by the name of Samuel Payne. Rich son of a bitch too. Not as much as the Buehlers used to be but close."

Alton nodded and stretched his neck. He knew that at one time there was a great deal of money to be had by the Buehlers, but Shamus had taken care of that. After asking Anderson to keep an eye on the place until he got there, Alton put his phone down and lay down. He had a great deal to do before meeting up with Shamus, and he wanted to be in top form when he found him. The son of a bitch was certainly going to wish he'd never met Alton Stockberry.

Chapter 11

Every time Samuel thought of Kennedy, his cock ached to find her and take her to bed. She wasn't going to be any happier with him now if he went to the kitchen and pulled her away again. This morning had been bad enough, he thought with a smile.

She'd been making something that had involved a great deal of flour. He'd seen her standing next to the counter with her short shirt and little shorts, and he'd walked up behind her and pulled her into him. After she'd moaned and leaned back into him, he figured that she was ready for him.

He'd never been so wrong in his life. Oh, she was ready for him, all right, but the rest of the staff was not. When they'd walked into the kitchen forty minutes later, it was to find the mistress and master of the house lying on the floor, both of them covered from head to toe in the white powder. The bowl had fallen at one point, but he couldn't remember why or when now. All he knew was that she'd screamed out his name several times and he'd bitten her twice.

"There's a call for you." He looked at Brigitte and tried to think what the hell she'd been saying. Her laughter made him flush. "You're deeply in love with her, aren't you?"

"More than I ever thought possible." She nodded to the phone when it rang. Picking it up, he made short work of the question that Aggie had for him and asked Brigitte to have a seat.

"Your missus won't even look at any of us." Samuel had the good sense to drop his head before he smiled like a fool. Brigitte apparently wasn't fooled. "Crow like that around her and I think she'll brain you."

"I didn't mean for her to be embarrassed. I wanted her, and there she was." He flushed at what he'd said, especially when she laughed again. "Christ, I'm going to be lucky she doesn't follow through with her first threat and put soft peter in my food."

"I doubt she'll do that." This time he was the one who was embarrassed, but she continued as if he wasn't bright red. "I would ask you for a favor, sir. It would be about the house you have in Ireland."

Samuel had had a solicitor send him what he had on Rose Manor. After going over the house plans several times, he'd finally had to put the blue print away and try to work on something else. The house was a great deal bigger than he'd first thought. He nodded at Brigitte when she smiled.

"I'd like...Peter and I were hoping that when the two of you go to see the house, you'd take us with you." He hadn't thought of going to see the place and was surprised by how eager he was.

"I'd like that very much. But if you go, it's to be a vacation for the two of you. You might as well get to see it the first time when I do." She nodded then shook her head. "You don't want it to be a vacation?"

"No, I mean yes, but it's not our first time there. Peter and I honeymooned there when we were younger. Much younger." She grinned at him as she continued. "I'd like to go back before my bones are too old to travel over those roads again. I've never been to where the missus is from, but I would very much like to see it."

"The *Lough Neahg* is only about twenty-five yards from the castle." He pulled out the map he'd been looking at, and had her come around the desk to look at it with him. "And look at this, the little burg that we're to keep has bed and breakfasts as well as a festival in the spring and fall that millions of people come to."

"Can you imagine living in a beautiful town like that one?" They both looked at the doorway when a short knock startled them. He watched Kennedy turn bright red again and felt badly for making her so uncomfortable. But Brigitte asked her to come in. "We were just looking at the maps to see where your ancestral home is."

She walked toward them, and he almost laughed. He'd not noticed that she'd changed and into something so hideous that he wanted to pull her into his lap and strip her down. If she thought wearing something so big was going to stop him from wanting her, she was very much mistaken.

She stayed on the other side of the desk from him. He didn't care. Her scent called to him, and he knew the exact moment that she realized it. Her nostrils flared, and he could feel her lioness as she moved along her skin. Samuel watched her struggle with the cat inside of her and hoped that she'd go out to the woods with him tonight and shift. She'd been so afraid since she'd been changed that she'd been begging him to wait. It was time.

"We have a boat that we used in the summer months. The cook would go out too to get fresh seafood for dinner sometimes." She pointed to Lough Neahg. "'Tis the longest river way in Ireland and boosts the best fishing. In the spring during the *Féile an Earraigh*, we'll let people come through the house to see what it's like. Shamus hated it, but it brought in a great deal of monies for the village. *Seanmháthair* had said that it gave a little back to the people by letting them be proud of the house that they cared for."

Samuel asked her to repeat the word for grandma several times before he felt he could say it without embarrassing anyone. Brigitte got it quickly, of course, and left them alone after saying it several times to help him. When she was gone he looked at Kennedy. She was upset about something.

"They're calling me 'lady.'" Samuel nodded and told her how they were calling him 'lord.' "I'm not. The lady of the house is my mother. I'm simply Kennedy."

There was more to this than she was saying right now, and he let it go by changing the subject. "I've been looking into this idea I have. It's about time I found another project, and this one is something that I feel we can work on together."

She looked at him, shocked. "You want me to work with ye? I thought that you said I was to behave and stay out of things."

He leaned back in his chair, knowing that this was going to come back and bite him in the ass soon. Samuel had said a great many things to her when he'd first met her, and now he was realizing what a fool he'd been.

"I want you to work with me on everything. I'm not going to tell you what to do or how to do things. As you've pointed out to me several times and quite loudly, you're capable of doing whatever you want, whenever you want." She flushed, and he laughed. "You can't be embarrassed, because you have a mind of your own, love. I'm beginning to think that you could run a business better than me."

"More than likely." She looked away, and he saw the sadness before she said anything else. Wanting to ask her what it was wouldn't work with her. She was a great deal like her grandmother and had to work things out in her mind before she'd talk to anyone about whatever was bothering her. When she looked at him, he could see the fresh tears, and went to the other side of the desk to sit beside her in the other chair.

"What is it, love? Are you homesick? Or is this because of this morning. I swear to you I never meant for anyone to catch us in that position. I saw you there and had to have you." She shook her head. "I love you, *mo ghrá*."

"You've been talking to someone. 'My love' is a very nice thing to say, but 'twill not get you directions if ye be lost in the great green world." He pulled her out of her chair and onto his lap. "My mother says she wants me to give her the stipend she's entitled to so she can never return to Ireland."

Samuel wasn't sure what to say, so he said nothing for several minutes. He knew that her mother wasn't happy with her eldest daughter. Every time the older woman spoke to Kennedy, Samuel found himself wanting to slap her. She never had anything positive to say to her daughter, and rarely had anything good to say about anything. Kennedy's brother Michael said that their fighting all the time was one of the reasons that Kennedy had gone to stay with their grandmother so much.

"If we give it to her, what do you think she'll do?" He felt her relief and wondered about it, but she got up and started pacing the room before he could touch on it with her.

"My parents never really got along. There were times when I wondered why they stayed together. I knew that my mother was a very proud woman, and my father could be...." She stopped pacing and stared at him with a frown. "He was a mon's mon. He liked to walk the estate once a week even if it was in the rain, and he would be known to muck out a stall with the help if they were shorthanded. She thought it beneath him."

"Your mother is a snob." He'd meant it as a joke, but she nodded. "And you think that she'll be embarrassed by me when I go there to run the estate."

"Nay, she thinks you'll do a fine job of it. She told my sister that you'd turn a profit on a nag if you wanted. She thinks it'll be me that'll embarrass you and the estate." Samuel started to laugh, thinking she had to be kidding. "I'll try not to mind, but I'm who I am."

"Thank God." She stopped pacing again and stared at him. "If you try to be something different, I'll paddle your butt. I love you just the way you are, and anyone that thinks differently will have to answer to me. You should hear the lawyer that I spoke to last night. He thought you being lady of the manor was the best thing that could have happened to it. He claims you're a great deal like your grandmother and that you might be a tad more fun to deal with."

"My grandmother is wonderful." He smiled at her defensive stance. "I'll knock anyone sideways that says differently."

"I think he might have meant that he was looking forward to working with us." She flushed, and he held out his hand to have her come to him. When she was settled on his lap he held her under his chin. "What do you want to do about your mom?"

"Ship her to another country?" They both laughed. "I doona. I was hoping we could work it out so that she'd be okay with me there, but…well, I doona think she wants to. Her mind is set."

"I'll have my attorney get with the estate one and we'll see what we can work out. I'm thinking that maybe after a few years she'll come around. Especially after we have a few children." He'd thought of her large with their child more and more lately and wanted to talk to her about it. But when she looked up at him, he could only think about how much he loved her.

"There's something else we need to talk about." He nodded as she continued. "I doona know what to do when my body screams at me."

Her lion wanted out to play. Samuel thought about saying that to her but didn't want to frighten her any more than she already was. Instead, he tried to think of what might work and started to tell her what he wanted to do to her when she was a cat.

"I want to chase you through the woods. You have a scent now that calls to my cat and he wants her to come out and play. He knows that you're tense about shifting, and he's trying to be patient, but he's not very nice, not like I am." She looked up at him with a grin. "I'm telling you right now that of the two of us, I'm the nicer. He wants to run you down and take you hard from behind while he sinks his teeth into your cat."

The plan was backfiring. He was so hard right now that he was sure that he wouldn't be able to walk without letting his cock free. When she shifted on his lap, he smiled when she moaned. There was no way they were getting out of this room without him taking her over the desk.

"I want you." He moaned at her statement. When she moaned, he shifted her around so that she was facing him on his lap. Her fingers wound into his hair, and she pulled his mouth to hers for a long, wet, hot kiss.

When she suddenly pulled away and stood up, he felt his cat snarl along his skin. Kennedy must have felt it, because she growled back low. Her cat seemed to dance along her skin until he was having a hard time telling her from the cat.

"I hurt." He nodded and stood up. Pulling her into his arms, his own cat started to take him, his need to have his mate almost as strong as Samuel's need.

"Come on, baby, let me take you outside, and we'll—" He stepped back when he felt her shift. The lioness took her master swiftly, and in seconds she stood where Kennedy had.

Christ, she was big. Samuel knew that an average lioness would weight over four hundred pounds, but Kennedy looked to weigh at least a hundred pounds more. Her fur was sleek and the lightest shade of tan he'd ever seen. Leaning closer to her, he realized she wasn't just tan but almost white.

I'm a lion. He nodded to her when she spoke to him. Samuel watched her carefully when she started walking around the room. As much as he wanted to laugh at her when she stumbled a couple of times, he didn't. She was much meaner than he was right now.

"We're going to go through the house, and I'm going to stay human until we're outside. Then we'll go to the woods, and I'll shift too." She moved along his legs, marking him with her scent. "Kennedy, you have no idea how beautiful you are right now."

He pulled out his cell phone, intending to take a picture of her, when someone knocked on the door to the office. Samuel wanted to tell her to go hide because he had no idea who it was when she growled low in her throat. When the door opened, Kennedy went to it and pressed her body against it to keep the door closed.

"Hello?" Her mother, Christ, now what. "I was wondering if I may have a word with your girlfriend. There is a matter of something we were discussing earlier."

Kennedy shook her head, and Samuel had a sudden thought of her mother seeing her daughter as a lion, and he had to put his hand over his mouth to keep from bursting out laughing. When Kennedy growled again, he moved to the door and stood just in front of it, hoping that she'd get the hint not to come in. Apparently her mother wasn't as pushy as her daughter.

"Kennedy is a little busy right now. She has a fur ball in her throat." The swipe at his leg made him wince, but Tisha didn't seem get his joke. "Can we discuss this later?"

"I would…I would like to settle this as soon as possible." She struggled with her accent, and Samuel wondered if he'd ever heard her let slip any of her brogue. Samuel glanced at Kennedy and knew that her mother had been the one to keep Kennedy from being herself about everything. "My daughter isn't happy with me, and I'm sure she's—"

"Kennedy." Tisha looked at him oddly. "Your daughter's name is Kennedy. You've called her everything but that since you've been here. Why?"

"I'm sure you're mistaken. And I'm well aware of what my daughter's name is. Her father, God rest his soul, had named her when I wanted her to have a feminine name, one more befitting our station. But he named her for him, and I've never understood her." She started to say something else, but Samuel didn't care to hear it.

"It's more than likely that you've never tried to understand her. She's vibrant and beautiful. Smart and a wonderful cook. Did you know that all the meals you've taken since you've been here have been cooked by her?" Her mother snorted. "You didn't enjoy them?"

"Do you see what I've had to put up with? She goes out of her way to embarrass me and show everyone that she's nothing more than a commoner. I had hoped that once she got herself wed that she'd straighten up, but she even refused me that." Samuel glanced at Kennedy as her mother continued. "You've no idea what I've had to endure because of her. All her *uafásach*, horrible ways have been nothing but an—"

"I think you've said enough." Samuel was tempted to open the door wider to show Tisha what her daughter was up to now, but didn't want to hurt Kennedy any more than he was sure this conversation had. He saw his own mom coming down the hall and knew that she'd heard most of what had been said. "I'll give you your stipend in the morning. In the mean time I'll have you taken to a hotel. There is no reason for you to subject yourself with us any longer."

"And my children, what will you do with them?" Her chin lifted, and he knew that she'd not included Kennedy in that statement. "And what of Shamus? Will you also give him his as well?"

"Shamus will get what he deserves. I'll make sure of that." She nodded, but Samuel would bet what he had planned for the man and what she wanted were two entirely different things. "Kaitlin will stay if she wants. Her fiancé will be here next week, and Michael has expressed a desire to learn a trade here in the States. I'm going to give him a job."

"He's my son, and he'll be with me. Kaitlin can do whatever she wants now that you've taken my daughter as your own, but I will have Michael with—"

"Back the fuck up or you'll not be getting a thing from me." Tisha's mouth snapped shut. "Now as I was saying. Michael will stay here. He's already asked about colleges, and I've got him an interview set up for next week with a friend of mine."

"Your mind is set then?" Samuel nodded. "My daughter? Did she tell you that I was a *uafásach* woman, and that's why you wish to treat me this way?"

"No, you showed me that all by yourself." Her stance went from rigid to ramrod straight. "Pack your shit up, Mrs. Buehler, you're about to experience hotel life."

When his mother was right behind Tisha, Samuel shook his head slightly at her. He knew that she was pissed off. His mother was very protective of what she considered hers, and she'd already taken Kennedy under her wing. When Tisha walked down the hall to the room she'd been given, Samuel opened the door for his mom.

"What a horrible person." Samuel nodded his agreement and looked over at Kennedy, who had curled up on the couch. Her cat seemed to stretch out over it as if she owned it. He smiled when his mother moved slowly toward her.

"Oh my, you're lovely, aren't you?" She stroked her fur gently, and he heard Kennedy purr. "That woman down the hall does not deserve you. And if I didn't think it would mess up that nice room, I'd have you go down there right now and have a bite or two of her."

"We were just going out for a run when she came to the door. I agree with you. Kennedy should have eaten her."

It would have left a bad taste in my mouth. Samuel laughed, as did his mother. He was slightly surprised that Kennedy could speak to them both, but he realized there was a great deal about Kennedy that was going to surprise him over the years. *Can we go out now? I want to see what you look like.*

"Oh that would be lovely. Go out and shift, Samuel, and when you do, I'll take both your pictures. I won't send it to you or anything like that, but I will have a print made. Yes, that would be so nice." He agreed, and he and Kennedy went down the stairs to the kitchen. When they entered, the only two people in the room were Butler and Brigitte.

"Missus, if you don't mind my saying so, you're a lovely cat." Kennedy walked to her and rubbed her head over her legs. "She's marking me."

When Kennedy moved toward Butler, he took a step back, but Kennedy wasn't having it. As soon as he was backed against the counter, she moved slowly toward him. Samuel tried to keep his own cat from snarling at the man.

"Sire, I didn't want to cause trouble. I think you should speak to the missus about marking other males." He cringed when she licked his hand. "Sire, you must ask her to stop."

I need to know I can find him. I have no idea why, but they're very important to me, and I want others to know that fucking with them is going to get them killed. Samuel told Butler what Kennedy had said. It took the staunch butler only a few seconds before he leaned down and rubbed his head along hers.

"I should like for her to keep me safe as well. Looking at her now makes me wonder if she would be able to take on that friend of yours that's the bear. Mr. Jonas would be so impressed with her, I think."

Kaleb was his friend from Illinois that was currently trying to buy a house in the area. Samuel couldn't wait for him to meet Kennedy either. As they moved out to the deck, he started pulling his shirt off, thinking about all his friends and what they'd think of his mate. He looked at Kennedy when she paced the deck.

"You should know that I'm still going to fuck you hard." She purred as she moved toward him. "As soon as I catch you I'm going to take you hard and fast. Then I'm going to shift with you and fuck you against a tree until you're hoarse."

You think so, do you? She snorted. *I'm going to mark you as soon as I chase you down. And when I do, everyone that comes within a mile of you is going to know that you belong to me.*

Christ, she was magnificent. He hoped his mother came out to take the picture soon because right now he was hard pressed to hold off from taking Kennedy on the deck where anyone could see them. But he had a feeling that she was going to give him a run for his money, and as soon as he shifted, he knew he didn't know the half of it. She was going to fucking kill him.

Mine, she whispered in his mind when the camera flashed. And when Mom said she had it, Kennedy leapt over the railing and was gone before he could catch his breath.

Yep, he was in so much trouble.

Chapter 12

Kennedy felt free for the first time in her life. Leaping over a fallen log, she laughed when she landed softly, startling a deer from his meal. The need to chase her seemed to roll over her, but she didn't want the creature to never return to this area so she took off in the other direction. There was nothing that didn't look different to her in his form.

The bark on the trees looked darker and rougher. She could see the tiny bugs racing over the skin of the tree like it was rush hour in Columbus. The moss growing on it looked like a small village where the green trees were reaching out to the sky. Leaping into the dirt because she could, she marveled at the snow that seemed to have a life of its own. Turning when she heard something behind her, Kennedy couldn't help but stare at Samuel.

You've been exploring, I see. She nodded, amazed that his voice sounded no different than it did when he was human. But that was where the similarities ended.

His mane was heavy and varied in colors of brown. Tans and golds fought with the darker of his fur until she thought that she could find every color of the earth on him. His face was elongated and full, strong and manly. She shivered when she thought of the last lion she'd come across, and Samuel came to stand beside her.

I'm not like him. She nodded, not sure how to tell him she was still afraid. *He's never going to hurt any of us again. You saved us from that.*

I know you're not like him. But you're…I never thought I'd want another one this close to me. He growled low when she rubbed her head over his massive shoulder. *Do you have any idea how amazing this is?*

I do. But seeing it through your eyes gives me a better understanding of how amazing it is. You're like a child getting her first brush with sex. She nipped at his shoulder, and he purred at her. *My cat wants you. Not nearly as much as I do, but he's getting close.*

Kennedy walked around Samuel, making sure she touched him as much as she could. She had no idea why it was important that she do it, only that she did. She supposed it had something to do with her wanting everyone to know he belonged to her, but she thought it was more. When he nipped at her shoulder as she'd done to his, he growled low.

Run. She didn't have to be told twice. Taking off in the direction she'd been looking, she nearly stumbled over some fallen brush. Before she could get herself up and moving again, he tackled her. They went rolling head over ass for several feet before they came to a stop. *You've made that much too easy. Run from me, baby. My cat needs the chase.*

This time when she started to run, she was much more careful. Knowing that he could smell her, she tried her best to stay to paths that she'd already taken, and avoided trees and limbs so they didn't get her scent. When she came upon a small brook, she walked down the middle of it carefully so as not to slip in the fast-moving water.

Twice she saw Samuel—once when he came close to where she'd entered the water, and again on the opposite side of where she was. Laughing quietly, she watched him sniff the air for her and wondered if she could do the same. Lifting her head up, she inhaled deeply and nearly fell back at the amount of input she got.

There was something rotting nearby. It was just to her left, and she decided to avoid that area, thank you very much. A deer was near her right, and she was with child. Trying something that Samuel said she could do, she reached out to the doe and asked her how she was feeling.

At first, she didn't think it had worked, but when she answered her back, Kennedy wanted to go and find her and hug her. *I'm fine, My Lady. You're new to the grounds. Are you the new mate to the lion master?*

I am. He and I will live here now, and you'll be safe from us and others. She told her that she'd figured that out when he'd never eaten her or her kind. *Are you a shifter or are you a deer?*

I am a deer. Laughter came through their connection. *My doe mate said that you were very beautiful and that you're very noisy. She said she hoped you didn't learn to be quieter so that we'd know you were always around. You nearly startled ten years off her life.*

I'm hiding from my mate. The doe laughed again. *I would like to catch him unawares, but as your doe mate pointed out, I'm not terribly good at this yet.*

I understand. He is about two sapling lengths from where you now sit. If you stay there, I will distract him for you. When the deer told her that he was now in front of her, Kennedy stood up and nearly screamed. He wasn't just in front of her but nearly atop her. When she leapt onto his back and took him to the ground, she laughed.

Got you. He rolled her off him and growled. Her entire body went hot with need, and he growled at her again. Rolling to her belly, she felt herself get wet when he came up behind her and pressed her into the ground.

I'm going to take you hard for that. She moaned at him, and he growled again. *Christ, do you have any idea how badly he wants to take you?*

Take me. Samuel, I need you both, please take me. He bit hard into her shoulder, and she snarled at him. It confused her at first that she'd want him so badly but still fight him. But when he fought her as well, she realized it was a game of sorts. As soon as he entered her, she cried out.

You're a virgin this way. I'm sorry, love, I should have remembered that. She moaned when he started to move in and out of her. *Christ, you're going to make him come soon. Be still.*

Nay, she needs this too. When he sank his teeth into her shoulder, she snarled again. The pain radiated through her body but was soon replaced by the most incredible euphoria. Her body moved with his, dancing their own tune until he yanked hard at her shoulder again.

He's marking his mate. When he comes inside of you, you're not going to be happy with him. He doesn't care if you come or not. She moved her hips until the lion hit the spot she wanted. He growled at her against her shoulder, but she didn't care. When he came, throwing back his head with a powerful roar, Kennedy joined him, coming as hard as him. But she needed more.

Shifting quickly, she rolled to her back and looked up at the lion standing over her. He was magnificent. His body was powerful and all hers. Kennedy begged Samuel to come to her, but the lion moved between her thighs.

Let him taste you. She shook her head as he moved to her pussy. *If you don't let him, he's not going to let me shift. You've no idea how badly he wants this. He wants both you and your lioness.*

Opening her legs, she bent her knees. Fear was slowly receding, but when he lapped at her pussy, she nearly came up off the ground. *More*, she begged him, and when he licked her again, touching her clit with his pebbly tongue, she screamed out her release and nearly fainted when he put his paws on her thighs to open her wider for him.

Kennedy came five times in quick succession. Each time he licked her, his tongue touching every part of her, she thought that she'd had enough. But every time, he'd give her more, take more from her until she was limp. When he backed from her, she whimpered, her body spent but needing more. As soon as the air tightened around her, she knew that Samuel was with her, and the moment he touched her, she was ready again.

"Christ, baby, I can't wait." She lifted her legs to her chest as he slammed into her. His cock was deep within her when she felt her own cat want to mark her mate. Letting just enough of her go to bite him, she cried out when Samuel bit her throat. Licking a path from his throat to his shoulder, she sank her teeth into him just as he roared out his own release.

Her own release pitched her over the cliff of darkness. It didn't just come over her but seemed to take her with a clap of thunder in a fast-moving car. When Samuel dropped on top of her, Kennedy thought about putting her arms around him but discovered it was too much effort and let go.

~~~

Shamus watched the house. There had to be something going on there, because every time he thought about going to the gate and trying to climb over it, another car would come in and he'd have to wait. Dinna this people have to work?

The small van with a moving company logo on the side startled him. He knew that the man of the house had only just recently bought the house and wondered if he was planning to move so soon. Shamus hadn't seen the house as yet but thought that when this thing with Kennedy was completed, he might offer to buy it from the man. It was just the kind of place he'd need, he was sure. The gates alone would impress anyone. Shamus looked up when the moving van moved out.

He watched the car behind it follow and was shocked to see his mother in the front seat of the car. She was crying. He could see that from where he was. Moving out of his hiding place, he watched the car and van move down the road toward town until he could no longer see it. Then he looked back at the house.

"Yer kidding me." Shamus looked down the street before looking at the house again. "Ye kicked my mother out of yer home? Ye bastard."

He wanted to storm the gate and demand the mon and tell him what had happened. Shamus wasn't even sure that's what did actually happen between the mon and his mother, but he would bet it. She could be a little on the grating side when she had a bone to pick with ye, but she was his mother. Shamus wondered about Kaitlin and decided that she was more'n likely still in the house. The man of the place would want to sell her off for more of a profit soon. Shamus went to his car and tried to remember once again how to get it moving.

Damned machines were everywhere here. If it wasn't a car it was something else he'd never had to deal with before. A microwave had given him fits just that morning. The hotel had provided it for him but with no instructions on how to use it. Samuel was a man who had things done for him, and fixing his food in the monster wasn't on his list of things he did. Or even wanted to learn. It had sizzled and popped so much that smoke came billowing out of it before he could get out his sandwich. The foil that had been wrapped around it was so hot that he'd burned his fingers. The hotel manager was not amused when Shamus had explained what had happened.

"You cannot use metal in a microwave. Even my five–year-old knows that." Shamus didn't care for his tone and told him so. "Then I would suggest you get your head out of your ass and learn how to use things before you burn down my hotel."

He'd told Shamus that any more incidents and he was going to be kicked out. When the man left, Shamus was tempted to put something else in the machine to piss him off but didn't have anywhere else to go. The money was nearly gone, and the horses that he'd bet on never came through. He had to play nice or would be living in the rental car he was now driving.

He followed the car to a little hotel, one much nicer than the one he was staying in. Waiting until the van left and his mother was inside, Shamus went to the door and knocked. When she answered, it took him several seconds to realize that his mother was this old woman standing in front of him.

"You left me there." His fist came out before he could think he shouldn't be hitting her. When she fell backwards, making enough noise to raise the dead, he walked into the room and closed the door behind him. She was just picking herself up when he clicked the lock home.

"How did you find me?" Shamus ignored the question to walk around the room. She was staying here. That much was obvious. And her things were not yet unpacked, so he knew that when she'd come here, it was because she'd been brought here. She hadn't been coming home.

"Why are ye staying here and not at the house?" She didn't answer him, and he turned to look at her. She cringed away from him when he knelt down to her level. "I asked ye a question. Answer me, Mother."

"He's given me my stipend, and I'm not going back to Ireland. And he's married your sister too, bloody fool." She sat up and then stood. "Your grandmother has given him Rose Manor too. Did you know that?"

"Aye, I'd heard that. But it won't hold. I'm the true laird of the house, and she well knows it." He heard her say something, and he turned back to her to ask her what she'd said.

"I asked you if you killed your father. You did, didn't you? Murdered your own father, and for what?" He didn't answer, because, frankly, he wasn't sure he could. All he could think about was they knew. "You didn't even get any more money when he died, and what you did, you've spent on nothing that would keep us safe. It's your responsibility to keep your mother safe."

"And what did you do for me, Mother? Did you once keep me safe from Father? When he took the strap to my ass, did you once tell him to stop? Nay, you did nothing."

"You deserved that. You'd killed off his best horse. Then you'd gotten that girl in the family way when you'd only been fourteen years old. What did you expect him to do, let you do whatever you wanted?"

"Yes," he screamed at her. "I'm his eldest, and he should have given me it all when I asked. Instead, he pampered Kennedy. Gave her what she wanted until she was smarter than me." He'd not meant to say that, but she only snorted at him.

"Smarter than you how? She's married to a man she hates, living in this cold, dirty country with a cripple as a mother-in-law, and what does she do? She tells me that I'm better off living here than with them." She looked around the room, and he did too. "I've no servants to speak of, no one to drive me about, and the money that I was given was nothing compared to what I had when your father lived."

"And I suppose that's my fault too." She lifted her chin, and he wanted to knock her back again. He'd never hit his mother before, only Kennedy and Kaitlin, but he found that it was an amazing feeling and wanted to do it again. When he moved toward her, she cringed from him, and that, too, made him feel better.

"You'll have to help me get Kennedy for Tailor. He wants her still, and though she's married, it'll not stop me from giving him to her. He wants his wife, and I need the money to pay a debt." His mother sat down and glared at him. "Will ye help me, Mother? I can make it worth your while."

"Samuel, Kennedy's husband, said that he'd take care of you. You need only to go and tell him to give you back your place in the manor and he'll have to give it to you. He isn't a smart man either." Shamus doubted that was true but only nodded. "He is taking care of Kaitlin too, having her man sent here for her. Michael is going to go to university here too. There's an interview soon for it."

University? Why would anyone think to go to more schooling? He'd barely made it through what was required of him before he'd figured out that he could simply pay someone to do his homework for him, and stealing the tests beforehand was simple enough as well. Shaking his head at the waste of it all, he flopped down on the chair across from his mother.

147

"I am hungry. Fix me something while I think." She got up to do his bidding, and he thought of something. "Why did you leave me there alone?"

"The money was gone, and I knew that the collectors would be by soon enough to get what they needed. You've done a piss-poor job of keeping the manor in our family. And since there be no brat from you, then I needed to keep what I could. The jewelry was taken from me, of course. Your grandmother said it was hers, and she wanted it back. She sent a man to the manor to get it just before we left."

That explained a great deal, thought Shamus. If his grandmother knew about the money problems the estate was having, she was well within her rights to take it from him and give it to the next in line. And since he knew that Kennedy couldn't inherit it, it would have to be her husband.

"*Seanmháthair* did this." His mother nodded. "When she figured out what I'd done, she'd done the impossible and married Kennedy off as I was trying to do."

"Yes, but she gave her something you'd never considered. The man loves her and will more than likely put up a fight if you try and take her from him." Shamus wasn't afraid of him. Money talked, and this mon would need it if he was laird of the manor. He asked his mother how much money she had, and when she asked him why, he grinned. "We need to pay him off. He'll give me what I want, and we'll all be back to the way things were before Da died. I'll be a better mon, and the manor will be ours."

"I've signed a paper." He looked at her oddly. "They had a solicitor there, and he had me sign off on a paper that said I'd never go back on my word. I cannot go back to Ireland so long as Samuel is Laird."

"He's not laird, I am." She moved back from his temper and he felt it flair again. There was something about having her afraid of him that made his dick hard. It was everything Shamus could do not to stroke himself. "I'll get this taken care of, and when I do, the contract you signed will mean nothing."

At least he hoped so. This husband of Kennedy's was proving to be a lot more difficult than he'd thought he'd be. First of all, for an American, he was proving to be a little craftier than he'd thought; and secondly, he was a good deal smarter than even Shamus thought himself to be. It was maddening the way things kept falling apart.

Moving toward his mother's bag, he was pulling out her wallet when she touched him from behind. His fist connected with her jaw almost in mid turn. When she lay on the floor again, he thought about hitting her again, but she wasn't moving, and he was sure that if she wasn't whimpering, he wouldn't enjoy it so much. Taking all her cash, Shamus decided that he'd go to the races again. Today should be his lucky day. Smiling, he thought it a good omen that the car started without him having to try several times. Today, he was going to win, and win big.

Just as he stepped out of his car, having only gotten lost once, he felt something jam hard into his back. The voice, quiet yet full of hate, told him not to say a word. Shamus started to turn and again whatever it was jabbed him harder.

"You'll get into that van and shut your trap. I'd like nothing better than to kill you right now." Shamus watched the big van come to a screeching stop in front of him, and he was shoved forward even before the door opened. As soon as he was tumbling in, the thing took off at great speed, and he was tossed to the rear.

"What's the meaning of this? I demand that you tell me this minute." The man in the passenger's seat laughed, and

Shamus felt his temper rise. "I will report you to the authorities if I doona get a straight answer."

The driver took a turn very hard, and Shamus was tossed about in the back again. He bumped his head twice before he was able to sit upright again. When he started to make more demands, the man pulled a gun out and told him to shut up.

"Stockberry sent me." Shamus felt his blood run cold in his veins, and he knew that he'd better think of a way out of this or he was as good as dead. "And before you open your trap again, just know that while I can bring you to him alive, you don't necessarily have to be in one piece."

Shamus didn't move, nor did he open his mouth. It was humiliating how these ruffians kept treating him this way. He was about to make all kinds of money, and now the opportunity was missed. He wondered if Kennedy had anything to do with this, and realized she wasn't that smart for all her education.

She'd pay. Shamus decided that as soon as she bred a child by Tailor she was going to meet with an untimely accident. And when she did, her dead husband would as well. Shamus would step in and raise her child until such time that he could get to his money as well. The boy wouldn't know what hit him. Shamus closed his eyes and let this plan develop. Kennedy and her offspring were going to pay for this.

Chapter 13

He watched her from the doorway as she worked in the kitchen. Samuel had reached for her an hour ago and found her missing from their bed. When he realized she was in the kitchen, he thought to come down and drag her back to bed with him, but her mind was working on something, and she'd blocked him enough where he could only find out she was upset but not about what. When she noticed him standing there, she paused in the process of pouring flour onto the counter.

"I was making a pie." He moved into the room and kissed her on the neck as he moved behind her. He went to the refrigerator to get something cold, thinking to pour it over his body when she continued. "I think that we should talk about yesterday."

"I agree." He sat down on the stool and drank deeply from the bottle of water he had to buy him some time. "You are the most beautiful lion I've ever seen. Even more beautiful than my mother, and she is very lovely."

"I'm talking about my mother." He nodded, figuring that's what she'd meant. "She means to not go back now, right?"

"I've already talked to her and sent her on her way. My lawyer drew up the papers saying that she'd get her money and not bother us again. She can't return to Ireland so long as I'm lord and you're the lady of the house." Kennedy started to say something, and he raised his hand. "That was her idea, not mine. But he put it in the contract for her all the same. She signed off on it this morning before being moved to her new place."

"Before we arose?" He nodded and watched her slice apples, seemingly not paying attention to what she was doing. "And she is now out of this house?"

"She wanted out, and I saw no reason to keep her here against her wishes. She is being watched by some friend of ours. Jimmy has two men on her now, and he'll report back to me if she does anything stupid." He was going to tell her that Shamus had gone to visit her, but the phone rang in the kitchen where they were before he could.

"Mrs. Buehler is being taken to the hospital," Jimmy said as soon as he answered. "I've got a man on Shamus because, before he went in, she was up and around now…Christ, who hits their own mother?"

Samuel told Kennedy what had happened, and she stood there staring at him for several seconds before she sat down. He couldn't tell what she was thinking about, but he was suddenly afraid for her. If Shamus was this unstable, there was no telling what he'd do if he found her.

"Send a few men over here to watch the house. And put one on David Patrick that's coming today." David was coming in today to see Kaitlin. She had asked him if he could come, and he'd thought it a good plan. Now he wasn't so sure. "Also, Dani, she'll need someone with her too. Michael is staying here, so he should be fine."

"On it. I've also got a few on a man that Shamus has been talking to. A man by the name of Alton Stockberry. He's the guy that bought the horses from Shamus and was arrested. I doubt if the man is any happier with Shamus than we are."

Samuel had his doubts too. After making arrangement to have Tisha put somewhere safe, Samuel hung up and watched Kennedy. She didn't look as if she'd moved since she'd sat down.

"Do you think Shamus meant to kill her?" Her question startled him, but he answered her truthfully.

"I don't know. I think your brother is a bit unstable, and if he's taking it out on your mother, something else is going on." She nodded and looked up at him. "What is it, Kennedy?"

"I think he killed Da. They'd been fighting before dinner that night, and when I'd asked Da what about, he'd told me that Shamus was spending his allowance as fast as he got it, and he'd gotten himself in trouble with his ways." Samuel went to her and knelt before her, taking her hand into his. "Da told me to be careful around him, that he no longer trusted him."

"Your grandmother said the same thing to me just a few days ago. She didn't mention the conversation, but she did say that she'd thought he'd killed him. And the fact that he'd had him cremated makes it seem more plausible." Kennedy nodded at him. "I wish I could tell you I'll find out for you, but there is no way now."

"Da said that he'd made inquiries to have Shamus put away. I'm not sure what he'd meant by that and hadn't really paid any attention. It wasn't until later, after Shamus had hit me badly enough to put me in the emergency, that I thought about it again. He isn't right in the head, is he?

"No, love, he isn't." She stood up then and went back to her crust. He stood up, then sat in the chair she'd been in. "What would you like us to do about him? He's hurt your mother badly, but the medic said she'd be fine if not for the headache."

"*Seanmháthair* will have to be called and told. I know that they only got along for Da's sake, but she should know." He told her about the guard that was on her when she'd left there. "She *ní bheidh sé an-mhaith.*"

Samuel was beginning to learn more and more of her first language. She would slip into it without thinking, and he'd have to try and figure it out or ask her. But when he asked her, she seemed to work harder at not letting herself say anything else, and he loved hearing her speak Irish to him. He figured that *ní bheidh sé an-mhaith* meant she wasn't going to like it. He had to agree. Neither would he.

As Kennedy called her grandmother, Samuel called Jimmy back. The man was in a better place to talk to him without the medics around and told him what he'd found. Jimmy made it very clear that he wasn't a big fan of Shamus Buehler.

"He hit her. Not once either, but a few times. And then he fucking robbed her. She was babbling about him not treating her well, and then she said that he was going to get Kennedy to Tailor. Then things would be all right. How the fuck is that going to be all right?" Jimmy ranted a little more before Samuel asked him where he was. "Let me call you back. Kaleb is calling me now."

Ten minutes later, Jimmy showed up at his house. When he asked him if he wanted to talk to him alone, he told him no, that Kennedy needed to hear this as well. In the end they and his mother and Kennedy's grandma joined them. It seemed that things with Shamus had just taken a step up.

"He's been taken by Alton Stockberry." Kennedy didn't know him, but Dani did. She stood up and then sat down twice before asking for something stronger than the tea she was sipping. Samuel handed her a bourbon neat, and she swallowed it down like she'd been doing it for years.

"Alton holds a great many of Shamus's notes. He's come to collect before. It's one of the reasons I asked Tisha for my jewels back. I had a feeling she'd give them to her son to buy his way out of this. It won't work, of course. He'd just get in deeper, but Alton isn't one to trifle with." Samuel asked her how much he was in for. "Nearly seven million. And he wants Rose Manor."

"Nay, he'll not get it." Kennedy went to him, and he pulled her into his lap. He'd noticed that she'd been doing that more and more lately, and he was enjoying it. But now she needed comfort, and he was going to give her all he could. "I'll do whatever it takes to keep him out of my home. Ye can't let him have it."

"He won't get it. Your father, God rest his soul, saw to that. He asked me years before his death to go to his solicitor with him. While there, we had the will changed as well as he sold me the manor so that it would be in my name and couldn't be touched by Shamus or his mother. Tisha would have sold it long before now had she been able to." This time Dani got up and poured herself another drink. "I, too, have had my will revised since then and have cut all, save you, from my money."

Kennedy sat up and was no doubt going to tell her that she'd better change it back when Dani took her hand into hers. The two of them were so much alike, both in looks and temperament, it was a joy for Samuel to see what Kennedy was going to look like in about fifty years. When Kennedy came back to where he was sitting, she didn't sit on his lap this time but close to him on the couch. He waited for Dani to continue.

"I've taken steps, financial ones, that will ensure that Kaitlin and Michael are cared for, but in a way that would only benefit them. Ye've never been one for asking for anything, so over the years I made sure ye had what ye needed." Kennedy mentioned her college. "Aye, that too. Your da could have paid for it if he wanted, but it was one of the stipulations to the house that I take care of you. He'd been giving me money to put aside for you so that when the time came...." She looked at him. "When the time came, she'd have her dowry for you."

"And this has to do with Stockberry how?" Jimmy flushed. "I'm sorry, My Lady, but if he has your grandson he's not going to give up until he has what he wants. And from what I've been able to piece together, he wants Kennedy as well as the house."

"He does. Alton has said as much to me when he'd seen her once." She sipped her drink as Dani continued. "He'll stop at nothing to get her either. Even going to far as to kill Shamus to bring her around."

"I'll not go to him. I doona know why he thinks that I'd come for my brother who near killed me once, but I'll not leave Samuel." Samuel took her hand and kissed it. "Ye've made me see what it's like to be loved, and I'll not do anything to bring you to harm."

"He'll not hurt me." Samuel looked at Jimmy. "Do you know where he has him held? And if so, how we can get him out?"

"I do. You're not going to like this. But Alton Stockberry is holed up right down the street from here. He and a man that I've never met are there now, and from what Jonas just told me, he's having a good time with Shamus." Jimmy looked at the women in the room and apologized. "I didn't mean to sound like I was happy about that."

They sat for nearly an hour trying to think how to take Alton out of the picture. When they decided that simply going in with guns blazing was the only way, he and the other men loaded up in the SUV and left for the other house. Samuel hated leaving Kennedy behind, but he needed her to protect her grandmother and his mom.

"If someone comes here, they're defenseless. Even Butler isn't trained to take on men who have no rules to follow and guns that can cut through a man even in a vest." She nodded at him, and he kissed her on the mouth. "I love you. Please never forget that."

"Aye, and you doona forget that I can kick your ass if you get hurt." He nodded and moved out of the house to the car. He turned and went back to her to kiss her again before hopping into the car. Christ, who would have thought that he'd be so in love that he'd rather stay at home than go out and kick some major ass?

"The house is being guarded by three patrols. Jonas said that two of them are out in the perimeter at all times while the others are in the house. There is also a motion detector in the house that he said was set up yesterday. But we don't have to worry about it." Jimmy smiled. "We installed it for him and know all the codes. Really is too bad we never showed him how to change that."

Samuel decided that his next project was going to be setting up an investigation team and working with Kaleb and Jimmy. They could do some major damage to the bad guys like this, and Samuel wanted to start something he could be proud of.

As they neared the house, Samuel kept telling himself that this was the only way to end this. And when he did, he was going to take his wife on a long vacation to Ireland and have her show him all there was to see. Then he was going to see if she'd have a baby with him. That would be the best thing he could have happen to him.

Going into the yard proved to be fairly simple. The guards were easily taken out, and once they were inside the house, the five men in there were dead before they ever knew what hit them. Samuel was moving toward the stairs when he felt something behind him. Before he could move to see who it was, something hit him in the back of the head and he was down. Christ, he thought as the pain tore through him, Kennedy was going to be so pissed off.

~~~

"Did you know how I ended up in a chair?" Kennedy looked at Summer and shook her head at her question. "Sam, Samuel's father, tossed me down the stairs. He'd been out with his girlfriend and I'd smelled it on him."

"I thought I was told that once you were mated that you'd never be able to hurt your mate." Summer nodded. "Then I don't understand. How was it possible for him to hurt you?"

"He'd been taking drugs. Plenty of them by the time Samuel was in grade school. He would beat him as well. Knock him around until he started to fight back." Kennedy got up to make her a cup of tea as she continued. "We'd been fighting again. Samuel was away at work and I'd been packing to leave his father. I was going to live with my son until I could find it in me to get out on my own. I'd never lived alone. Going straight from my family's house to Sam's. I wasn't sure I could do it."

"You would have or died trying." Kennedy sat the container of sugar in front of the other woman as she heated the water and the cup. "You were leaving him you said. I guess Samuel was going to help ye out?"

"He was. I'd called him that morning and told him what I was doing. By the time he'd gotten there, I'd been hurt. I'd been…Sam had left me there lying on the floor and I couldn't get up, couldn't move at all. Samuel came into the house to help me and found me in a mess at the bottom of the stairs and his father gone."

"He went to prison? Your husband?" Summer shook her head. "Then where did he go? The police would have been called to the house."

"No. Pride takes care of pride, and by then the males of our pride had found out about other things that Sam had been involved in and had taken steps to have him ousted. Then there was the house." She looked out the window as she talked about what her life had been with her husband. "He'd used the house as collateral for his drugs. Several times as a matter of fact. By the time that Samuel had figured it out and paid it off, his father was long gone and a wanted man by the pride and several banks. It took Samuel nearly a year to get things straightened out and another one to get the house and everything in his name. By then he had a buyer for it all and sold it the very next day. We moved here the month before it was final and Samuel became a nomad from the pride."

"He's alone then." Kennedy knew that there were no other lions around. She just didn't understand that it was by choice and not him having his own pride. "Will he join another pride then?"

"Doubtful. He can take over one or form his own. It's harder for a single male to do so, but it's happened. Or he can choose to live his life as he is. I think that given the things that he's been involved in lately that he might form his own pride, but not necessarily with lions. He seems to be the leader of a great many different kinds of shifters."

"Jimmy and the man they call Jonas?" Summer nodded. "There are more, too. I met a deer in the woods that said she felt safe here."

"There are no deer shifters here." Kennedy explained to her about the one that had helped her the day she had shifted. "You spoke to a non-shifter? Does Samuel know this?"

"Nay, I dinna think to tell him. I didn't know it was wrong." Kennedy got up when the pot whistled and poured hot water in the cup to warm it, then put the tea ball into the warmed cup and poured more hot water over it. When she set the timer, she looked at Summer, who was smiling at her oddly. "What?"

"You're a true Irishwoman, aren't you?" Kennedy didn't understand, but before she could comment, Summer continued. "The fact is you can speak to other shifters because it's something that Samuel can do. It's only right that you would be able to do so as well. But if what you're saying is true—and I've no doubt that it is—you've taken his gift and changed it to something more. Oh my, Kennedy, the possibilities that have come to you are outstanding."

Kennedy didn't understand what the big deal was and nearly said so. But then she nearly doubled over with pain and had to lean hard against the table when another pain tore through her head and dropped her to the floor. Samuel was in trouble.

Blood poured from her mouth and nose as she tried her best to stand up. She needed to get to him, but she was being held down and someone was screaming at her. Letting her lion talk to her, she found that she was just as worried and wanted to be let out to get her mate. Kennedy had to calm her before she could stand up again.

"It's Samuel, isn't it?" Kennedy nodded and had to run to the trashcan to throw up. She lifted her head just as Summer handed her a wet wash cloth. "Concentrate, love. Close your eyes and reach for him. See if he can tell you where he is."

She tried to do what she'd been asked but all she hit was a wall. And it was full of blood and pain too. When she tried to reach out to something else, anything that might know where he was, she found a human nearby. Kennedy entered his mind to see what he knew.

"They're no longer at the house. This one is smaller, there are few windows and there seems to be...." The man turned then and she saw Jimmy and Kaleb. "They're hurt badly but tied up. Kaleb has a knife wound in his chest and Jimmy's face is bruised. Both of them are tied up."

"Do you see Samuel?" Kennedy realized that she was seeing what the man was and thought about Samuel to see if he'd go look for him. There was nothing in the man's mind about her mate, so she didn't know how to have him look for him.

"Nay. Nothing." The man started to move from one room to another and she saw the kitchen. "'Tis no house but a restaurant. The stove is gas and had...eleven burners on it. I see a walk-in and...and there is an industrial dishwasher." She came across something on the floor, and the man looked at it long enough for her to see what it said. "They're at the Blue Diamond. Do you know where that be?"

"I do. It's on Jefferson, but it's closed. I think the health department closed it up." Kennedy still hadn't found Samuel, but she knew where the others were. She was moving to the door when Butler stopped her.

"I'll be going with you, missus. There is a time when I was a soldier, but now I'm a cook." He handed her a handgun, and she handed it back. "You'll take it and use it if you need to. Humans have them, and if there are any in the house, then we'll shoot them. If that fails, then you can go to plan *B*."

"And what is plan B?" He smiled at her, and she felt a shiver run down her spine. He was sort of scary when he looked like that.

"Then, My Lady, you eat them."

Chapter 14

Samuel felt as if he was going to be sick. His head didn't just hurt but felt as if he'd been dropped on it several times, and then someone had used a jackhammer on it. He lifted his head up when he heard a noise. His arms were chained above his head and his legs were shackled to the floor. He was truly fucked.

Reaching beyond the walls, he found that other than the guard outside, there was no one else around. As he didn't have the strength to try much harder than that he decided that whoever else was here could come on in and have at him. He was just too exhausted. And every time he tried to get in touch with Kennedy, he felt his head start to hurt more until he either had to stop or pass out. And being awake might keep him a little safer. The sound of the lock being turned had him drop his head and go limp.

"I told you not to hit him the second time. She won't come if she finds out he's dead." Samuel knew that voice but for the life of him couldn't place it. "She's a tad on the stubborn side, her brother said, and if she figures out we've lied to her, she'll hurt me."

"Christ, do you always whine this much?" The other man he didn't know but listened to him because he seemed to be in charge. "Alton said we were to get him at all costs, and that if he gave us any shit, we was to break him."

"What do you suppose that means?" Samuel wanted to roll his eyes and chuckled to himself when the other man apparently slapped this man. "That fucking hurt. You hit me again and I'll break you."

"You're a moron, did you know that? To break him means we do whatever necessary to get him to cooperate with Alton. We have to get him to tell his wife that he wants her to come and get him."

"I thought that we didn't care if this guy lived or not so long as we had the woman." Another slap and the man must have hit something hard this time. "I swear to Christ you hit me again and I'm going to be pissed off."

Samuel wished that he could see these two. They had to be the dumbest two beings he'd ever had the misfortune of being around. When the door sounded again, he waited for several minutes before he lifted his head again. Thankfully, he was alone.

His body was healing itself but not as quickly as he'd hoped it would. There was no way for him to shift because of the chains at his wrists and ankles. His cat was bigger, but there was no way for him to break the chains while shifting. He'd lose his hands and feet if he tried it now. Trying to yank the chains out of the wall didn't work either because it was too noisy as well as he was still weak from blood loss. He looked at the window when a bird suddenly appeared.

When it jumped down from its perch and landed near him, Samuel was too shocked to do more than watch it. The little robin seemed to be very nervous and kept looking back at the door, then at him. Hopping back and forth on his tiny feet had Samuel thinking that there was something wrong with it, and when he flew up and landed on his shoulder, Samuel knew it.

You're the master lion? The voice in his head nearly made him cry out because as surely as he was standing there he was sure the robin had spoken to him. *I've not got all day, are you the master lion or not?*

I am. The robin nodded once and flew to the window and sat there. *The missus said that if you have any information she can use she'll come and fetch you.*

Kennedy? The bird nodded. *You're not a dream, are you? Kennedy actually sent you here to question me about where I am.*

Again the little bird nodded. *She said to tell you that you've got to help her, that she can't...no that's not right, canna she said she canna help you.*

He wanted to ask the little fellow if he knew why she'd sent him a bird to help but knew that the blow to his head was worse than he thought. He was conversing with a bird, and then he was going to help him somehow.

I don't know where I am. Can you go out and look around and come back to tell me? If you see some landmarks I can maybe identify them for you. The bird took off when the lock on the door sounded. Samuel didn't bother trying to look weak this time. He'd been talking to a bird. He was pretty sure he was off his rocker.

"Hello, Payne. I'm Alton Stockberry." Samuel didn't say anything because he wasn't sure that whatever came out of his mouth wouldn't be gobbledy goop. "You've been hurt badly, I'm afraid. It wasn't my intentions to harm you in anyway."

"Then what the hell did you mean to happen when you send in a bunch of goons to bring me to you? And what the hell for? My wife?" Samuel snorted. "She's mine."

"Very unfortunate that you've married her. I did intend to have her all to myself." Alton leaned against the wall and smiled at him. "I can pay you dearly for her. She's quite a beauty, but not really up to your usual standards now, is she?"

"I don't have a standard."

"Precisely. Which is why I think that we can come to an agreement, you and I. I'll give you four million dollars for her. That's just about what her brother owed me until his most unfortunate accident. And you can walk away without any more bruises to your body. Or...." Alton smiled again. "I simply take her from you, keep my millions, and you die."

The bird came back. For some reason Samuel was in a more open frame of mind. When the bird told him about the train tracks and the waterways, Samuel had a better idea where he was but needed just a little more.

The tracks, can you see if there's a restaurant there? It would be a tall building with a parking lot out back and to the left of it. The name of it is Steak Tracks.

I can't read or tell left from right. I'm a bird, not a human. Samuel apologized and asked him if he could tell if the restaurant had a railing out front. But before he could finish describing the place Alton hit him.

"I think you should pay attention to me. Your life may very well depend on it." Alton went back to where he'd been standing and pulled out a gun. From where Samuel was he knew that the man wouldn't miss him. The bird came back and said yes there was. Samuel knew just where he was.

"I think you've underestimated my wife. She's very resourceful and will find me." Alton brought the gun up to his head and pressed it between his eyes. "You kill me and she'll tear you apart. And I'm not making an idle threat."

Samuel was surprised when the gun went off. The pain radiating from his belly made him think that he'd been kicked, but when he looked down, there was blood blossoming from his shirt and over his pants. He looked at the bird and told him just where he was.

Tell her to hurry. Tell her that I love her and want to spend the rest of my life with her. The bird nodded and flew away. Samuel watched as Alton stepped out of the room and the lock clicked. Samuel called him back. "You'd better be ready for her. When she gets here, she's not going to be too happy with you that you've shot me."

"You thinking she can get to me without me allowing it? I've been in the business of keeping myself safe for a good long time, Payne. I'm pretty sure I can handle one woman." Samuel laughed, and Alton suddenly looked a little less sure of himself. "You think I fear her?"

"You'd better. Because you've no idea what kind of woman she is. And what she can do to you once she finds me. And she will, make no doubt about that."

Samuel sagged against the chains. He was in such pain and was losing blood fast. He hoped that he'd not completely lost his mind and that the little bird was going to help him. Glancing at the window again, he hoped that in some way she'd been able to speak to the bird and was right now coming for him. Samuel closed his eyes and did something he'd not done in decades. He prayed.

~~~

They were moving as a group toward the house where Samuel was. The rescue of the others had gone better than she'd hoped. Only one dead, and both Kaleb and Jimmy were now up and about. They had both shifted within seconds of having them untied and now they wanted vengeance. Jimmy was driving the car they were in.

"He'll be fine." She nodded but didn't say anything. "You saved us; you'll save him. He's a lot tougher than he looks."

"The robin said he'd been hurt. And he thought that he'd been shot again before he came to me. How long can he survive with a bullet hole in him?" Jimmy didn't answer, but that was telling enough.

Shamus was dead. She'd come upon his body before anyone else and had stood there staring at him rather than seeing if he was really dead. When she'd been shoved out of the way by one of the other men that had come with her, Butler had taken her into the hallway and held her hand. She was sure he'd said something to her, but for the life of her she had no idea what it had been. There was just so much damage done to him for her to—

"Don't." She looked over at Jimmy when he'd barked at her. "Don't think about your brother. Shamus got himself into this and he had to know that it was going to end about like this."

Kennedy nodded. "I know that, and I understand that he brought this all on himself, but he was still my brother."

"Yes, a brother that sold you out along with his own family." Kennedy looked at Jimmy and knew that he'd been hurt like Samuel had by his family.

"Who hurt ye?" He glanced at her, and she saw the pain. "Who hurt ye from your family that turned you so bitter?"

"It doesn't matter. I'll never set myself up like that again where a person can dig my heart and soul out without a backward glance." Jimmy slowed down to turn into the parking lot where they were headed. "You keep with me. I know you want to find Samuel, but he'll never forgive either of us if you get hurt."

"I'm going to find him, and then I'm going to kill Alton. If the man is here, he's mine." Jimmy looked at her for long moments after he turned off the car. She had no idea what he saw there, but whatever it was he nodded to her. She slipped out of the car when he did.

The abandoned building was much bigger than she'd thought it would have been from the pictures they'd found on the Internet. It had looked like it was single storage, but it was actually three levels and a basement. Robin had said that there was a window almost to the ground where Samuel was and that he'd been able to see down into it. That meant that Samuel was in the lower levels, not the upper. As the others entered the building, she moved slowly from window to window, peering in to see if she could see Samuel.

A noise behind her had her still. She knew that dressed the way she was no one could see her without a light. She turned slowly, pulling the scarf up over her face until just her eyes were uncovered. She saw the man before he did her.

Moving slowly across the lot, she moved up behind the man and grabbed him around the head. She had only meant to shut him up in the event that he tried to warn the others, but he'd struggled too much and she had to work harder to hold him. She heard the snap and he went limp in her arms. She nearly cried out when she realized she'd killed him.

What's happened? Jimmy's voice resounded in her head. *Where are you? Have you found Stockberry?*

No, she told him, debating on whether or not to tell him about the man she'd killed. In the end she told him that she'd had to subdue a man. *I had to shut him up.*

Well you did that. He was laughing at her, and she wanted to smack him. *Stay out of trouble, will you?*

Kennedy decided to ignore him. She was moving toward the building again when she felt someone else coming toward her. What the hell was this? Grand Central? Moving deeper into the shadows, she tried to think where the person was coming from when they said her name.

"Kennedy, is that you?" She moved deeper into the shadows, not believing who it might be. When Tuck laughed slightly, she came out knowing that laugh of his anywhere.

"Mr. Savage?" He moved toward her, and then she saw Amy. They hugged her into their arms even as she saw the man coming toward them all.

After telling her to be quiet, Tuck moved away from her and shifted. He'd done that before to show her that he really was a bear, but this time was different. She knew that he was going to hurt someone.

He never made a sound as he swiped at the man. Kennedy was glad it was dark, because she was sure that he'd sliced the man's throat open by the sounds of it. When he moved back toward her and Amy, she could smell the blood.

"You're a lion." She nodded at Amy. "We came when we heard about the woman that had been killed on the property. I don't suppose you know who she was, do you?"

"It was me. I wasn't killed but…. Can we please find Samuel first? And I have to kill a mon who tried to hurt him." The Savages looked at one another and then at her. "There's a man, his name is Alton Stockberry and he took Samuel from me."

"Samuel Payne?" She nodded, suddenly very afraid they were going to tell her that they'd already found him and he was dead. "Christ, girl you sure know how to pick them. Let's go and find your man."

Amy moved back just as a man came around the side of the building. His scent hit her first, and then she smelled Samuel on him. She moved forward slowly and felt her lion crawl along her skin. Tuck whispered for her to go steady, but she knew this was her prey.

"Where is he?" He took a step back when she spoke right next to him. As he reached for something in his coat, she grabbed his arm and pulled it behind him and a gun dropped to the ground. "Where is Samuel?"

"Ah, Kennedy, what are you doing? Don't you know that there are several of my men walking around here just itching to kill someone?" He tried to pull away from her, but she was stronger. "Let me go, my dear, and we'll try to be reasonable about this."

"I'm in no mood to be reasonable with you. Where is my husband?" Tuck stepped in front of them, but he made no move to take the man from her or even to tell her to let him take care of it.

"Your men? They're dead. I killed one, and Kennedy here broke the neck of the other. Damn fine job she did too. Snapped it right at the base where the bone is the easiest." Tuck laughed as he continued. "I'm thinking she'll do the same to you if you don't tell her where her husband is."

"I don't know what you're talking about. Why would I know where Samuel is?" She nearly pointed out that she'd never said his name about the time that he realized his mistake. As soon as he did, he moved so that she was no longer holding him. Her cat decided that she'd had enough waiting and pulled her under.

Her claws raked down his belly until she touched his thighs. The scent of blood nearly drove her over the edge when he staggered away from her. As soon as he reached for Amy and started to pull her toward him, Kennedy leapt at him and snapped her powerful jaws around his throat. Before she could think that she might want to back off, she tasted his blood as it filled her mouth. She started to pull away when Tuck put his hand on her back.

"Finish him. If you don't, he'll come after you again and again until he harms what is yours." She snarled at him but felt Alton's heart start to slow. "Hold him there, love. If you don't, I'll have to kill him myself for touching my mate."

Snarling again, she shook her head and felt his head loosen from his shoulders. When she lifted her body from his, she watched in horror as Alton's head rolled away and landed in the grass nearby. She looked at Tuck when he reached for her.

"Steady, girl. Calm your cat." Kennedy felt her power surge over her and the need to kill again. "Come on, Kennedy, tell her that she needs to think that finding Samuel is imperative."

Slowly by degrees, she felt the cat calm. She was still pissed off, but she wasn't ready to murder the first thing she saw either. When Tuck let her go, she looked at Amy, who was holding her arm in the crook of her other arm.

Did he do that to you? Shock registered on her face, but she nodded. *I'm sorry that he hurt you. I never meant for anyone to get hurt.*

"You can talk to us?" She looked at Tuck and told him she could talk to anything. "Christ, girl I'd keep that little tidbit to myself. There are beings out there that would kill to have you. All species?"

Everything. They don't even have to be as shifter. I talked a robin into helping me for more food in his feeder through the winter months. He shook his head and bowed before her. *What are you doing, get up.*

"You're very special, Kennedy. More so than we ever already believed you to be." He pulled Amy to him and held her. "Does Samuel know?"

Nay, he's been a bit busy since I figured it out. She stood up suddenly and ran to the building. She needed Samuel and sitting there talking wasn't finding him. Jimmy came out of the building just as she was rounding the corner.

"I've found him. He's hurt bad and might…he needs to shift, but he won't until he's seen you. But he needs to do it soon." She nodded and he smiled at her. "Do you have any idea how much he loves you?"

Not nearly as much as I love him. As she entered the building she wondered how much help she'd be to him when she was a cat. But just as she was about to go where Jimmy pointed, Amy handed her a pair of pants and a shirt.

"It'll be big on you but you should be able to keep it on." Nodding her thanks she headed to the basement and went into an empty room. The cat was ready to let her be human again and Kennedy pulled on the clothes quickly. Going to the room where Samuel was had her fighting tears. He looked very bad.

"There's my girl." Samuel's voice was hoarse and soft. She went to him when he looked at her, and she knew that Jimmy was right. If he didn't shift, he would die.

"What the fuck is wrong with you? Ye wanting to have me carry ye out on me back too?" The others in the room backed up. "Look at ye lying about here like there is nothing to do. Ye've a house full of people at the house waiting on ye to show up, and there you lay." He started to say something to her, but she snapped at him. "Shift, damn you."

Chapter 15

Samuel opened his eyes and looked around the room. He'd been here for two days now, and he was ready to murder someone. When the door opened, he was both glad and disappointed it wasn't Kennedy. She'd been bossing him around since she'd called his beast.

"Kennedy is cooking again." Jimmy sat in the chair next to the bed and laughed. "She's going to make everyone here as fat as a goose if she keeps this up."

"I've told her countless times that she needs to hire a cook so she doesn't have to do it any longer." Jimmy shook his head and laughed harder. "She's not going to do it, is she?"

"I'm sure she will eventually, but right now I think it's the only thing that's keeping her from going over the edge. She's a mite on the tense side." Samuel knew that. He could feel it every time she spoke to him. And especially when she was in the room with him.

"I don't want her upset, Jimmy. You have to help me fix this for her."

Jimmy handed him a file, and he opened it. There were pictures of two dead men as well as the house he'd been held in. He looked at his friend when he didn't explain.

"She killed Stockberry, as you know, but what you don't know is that she killed another man first. Snapped his neck when he tried to call out. I didn't know that at the time because she'd only told me that she'd subdued him. I thought she'd tied him up." Samuel looked at the man lying on the ground with his head at an odd angle as Jimmy continued. "She killed Stockberry when he tried to get away from her. Tucker and Amy Savage told me that she'd shifted, too, as if she'd done it all her life."

"Why are you telling me this?" There had to be a reason. Jimmy never told something straight out when ten hours would do better. "Get to the point."

"She can talk to animals." Samuel thought of the bird and felt his heart start to beat harder. He'd never mentioned that to anyone and was almost afraid to tell Jimmy he already knew.

"A bird came to me while I was in that basement." Samuel looked away and at the snow coming down outside his window. He didn't want to see his friend's face when he told him. "I thought I was out of it and couldn't think straight. But he'd said that Kennedy told him to come to me."

"Tucker Savage and his wife came to me just after you were brought here. He said that he was afraid for her if anyone found out. He said that what she can do is a gift but others will try to take her for it." Samuel nodded, having talked to the big man last night. He'd never mentioned Kennedy's abilities but had asked him if he and his mate could join their pride. Samuel told Jimmy what he'd said.

"So are you going to do it?" Samuel looked at him, frowning. "You could do it. Have a pride of all kinds of shifters. You can already speak to all of us. So can Kennedy."

"Kennedy can do what?" She came into the room as if they'd summoned her. She was carrying a large tray that Jimmy took from her and sat across his lap. Samuel looked down at the food on it.

"Who are you feeding? Or should I say how many did you expect to feed?" He'd been short with her and Jimmy knew it too. When he stood up and moved toward the door, Samuel had a feeling that he was about to get his ass handed to him on a platter. When the door shut, he looked at her.

"I'm sick of being in this bed, and I'm fucking sick to death of everyone treating me like I've got some sort of fatal disease." She took the tray from him and walked to the door. "You leave this room and so help me I'll find you and beat your ass."

She didn't even turn. Opening the door one-handed, she moved into the hallway and stood there for several seconds before she turned. When she sat the tray down on the floor, he thought maybe she'd talk to him now. But when she picked up the glass of juice and threw it at him, he almost didn't dodge in time.

"What the fuck was that for?" Next came the cup with hot tea. He knew it was hot because it burned him on the leg just before the thing shattered over his head. Her aim was getting better. When the plate hit him in the chest, he knew he was in trouble. After she'd hit him once, it was all-out war on her part. Another cup hit him in the head, a platter of sausage hit his leg, there were tomatoes hanging in his hair, and he had egg all over his face. When he stood up, she picked up the tray and held it like a bat. He moved slowly toward her.

"You hit me." She nodded but didn't drop the tray. That's when he noticed the tears. "Are you really that pissed at me?"

"I've been trying for two days to leave you alone but you kept calling for me. I don't want to be here." That stopped him. "She's blaming me and I dinna do it."

"Who is?" Then it occurred to him. "Your mother? She's blaming you for...for Shamus's death? That wasn't your fault."

"She said if I had simply done what he said then he'd be alive and everything would be fine. Mother said that she knew that Shamus killed Da and that she had thought it was the right thing to do. Da, she said, wasn't happy with their marriage and would have sent her away. How is that my fault?"

"It's not." Moving slowly, tiny steps at a time, he made his way through the mess to her. She still held the tray, but it was sagging at her shoulder, and her knuckles were no longer white. Reaching out, he pulled it from her fingers and dropped it to the floor. Pulling her to him, he held her while she sobbed.

"I dinna do anything to Shamus. When I went to tell her he was dead, she looked at me and asked why it couldn't have been me instead of him. He was her boy." Kennedy looked up at him, and he could see the pain in her eyes. "I'm her daughter, doesn't that count for something?"

"I'm so sorry, love." She continued to sob against his chest as he held her. When Butler came to the doorway, he shook his head at the man, and he nodded once and left. Turning them, he moved enough to shut the door and picked her up into his arms.

Samuel held her until she stopped crying. And then long enough for her to fall asleep. Lifting her closer to him, he stood up and started for the bed but smiled at the mess there. Turning, he went to the door again and into the hall. Taking her to the bedroom next to theirs, he put her on the bed and stripped off her soiled clothing. When she was naked, he pulled off his own clothes and crawled into the bed next to her.

"You could have told me you wanted me. Pissing me off by throwing food at me wasn't a way to a man's heart." He whispered that he loved her and pulled her into his arms. Within minutes he was asleep.

~~~

Kennedy woke screaming. She grabbed onto the sheets and pulled herself up to see Samuel between her legs. He was grinning at her like he'd just won the lottery.

"I thought you'd enjoy that." He moved down her body again, lifting her leg up and kissing her knee. "I could smell you laying there all warm and sexy."

"I do not smell sexy." She moaned when he nipped at her calf. "Stop that. I'm upset and I don't need you muddling me all up with your body touching mine."

"You mean like this?" He ran his finger up her thigh to her pussy and entered her slowly. "You're very wet and you do smell like sex. And taste it too. Do you have any idea how long I've been wanting to do this?"

"You were supposed to be resting. Your mother said that you needed rest and not to be stressed out." He laughed. "I was trying my best to leave you to your own."

"You did too. And now I've got to make up for lost time. I do hope you're up for the challenge." She moaned again as he continued to move in and out of her, stretching her more and more. "You should see what I can when you're enjoying yourself. Your nipples are hard and pink and your body is flushed with need. The beads of sweat that are across your forehead are even sexy to me."

"Samuel, please, stop teasing me." She rode his fingers, hoping to get him to touch her clit. If he did, then she was going to come again. She wanted that.

"I want to taste you again. I so love the way you fill me with your cream and then when you come you flood my mouth with your juices." He moved to her again, leaving her leg over his shoulder. "Then when you come…oh, I don't know, seven or eight more times, I'm going to fuck you."

His mouth set off a quick climax the moment he covered her. Begging him for more, she curled her fingers into his hair and tried to guide him to where she wanted him, but he wasn't having it. He lifted her up and slid his hands beneath her. She screamed when he suckled her clit hard into his mouth.

"That's it, baby, only seven more to go and I'll enter you. I'm going to fuck you slow and easy before I mark you again." Whimpering, she tried to get him to hurry, but he was playing again.

For what seemed like hours he teased her, ate at her, and gave her just enough release to make her want more. When her body was limp, she begged him again to stop. This time he lifted his head.

His eyes were so dark that she knew that his beast was there. Reaching down to touch him, she watched as he sank his teeth into her wrist. Her body felt like it was poised on the edge of a sharp knife and either way she fell was going to be fantastic. Samuel sat up now, leaning back in his toes and fisted his cock.

"I want to taste you." He shook his head and started to crawl up her body. "Please, Samuel, I want to feel you come down the back of my throat. I want to have you in my mouth."

"Next time. I swear, next time. Right now I'm in so much pain I can hardly stand it. The minute I enter you, I'm going to come." Nodding, she opened her legs for him, bringing her knees up to her chest. "That's it, baby, give it all to me."

He moved into her slowly. Inch by incredible inch, he filled her. Sweat dripped from his body to hers and mingled with the sweat of her own need. When he was buried as deep as he could be, she shifted her hips and he surged forward.

Kennedy reached down and grabbed his ass. The muscles were tight and strong and pulling him deeper into her, she cried out when he touched her spot that only he knew about. The next time he moved, she dug her heels into his thighs and rocked up. Samuel took her breast into his mouth and bit her.

"I'm coming," she screamed at him. "Christ, Samuel, I'm coming." Her body bowed up of its own accord, and when she released, stars danced in her vision and she bit into his shoulder. When he did the same, sank his teeth into her throat, she cried out again, her body seemingly coming apart above her and coming back together with the power of a bomb. Screaming again, she felt her cat roar, and when Samuel lifted his head and roared too, Kennedy lost consciousness.

Kennedy woke slowly. She heard the thump-thump of Samuel's heart under her ear and smiled. There was something very nice about waking this way. Of course the other way had its merits as well. Smiling, she moved her hands down his body until she found his cock. His hand wrapping around her wrist had her looking up at him. He was smiling at her.

"As much as I'd like to continue your thought process, Butler needs to talk to us." She pulled away and moved down more until her fingers brushed over him. "Kennedy, if you don't stop now, the people waiting in our living room are going to know that I've come again. I'm reasonably sure they might know what we're doing anyway."

"How would anyone know that?" She sat up, forgetting about her nudity until he pulled her back down and moved over her. "I thought we didn't have time for this."

"We don't, but you're making it very difficult to keep on track." He kissed her quickly and rolled out of the bed. He stood there so hard, his cock straining from his body, that she moaned and licked her lips. "Stop that. Damn it, woman, the Pride Council is downstairs and Butler says that they're not happy with us. If I take the time to let you do what you have in mind, we're going to be later."

"I don't care." She crawled to the edge of the bed and sat on it. Pulling him toward her, he didn't resist but let her. When his cock was near her mouth, she licked him, taking in the pearly cum that was at the tip. "You taste amazing."

As she took his thick crown into her mouth, he rocked forward. Kennedy had never done this before and was surprised at how much she was enjoying it. Wrapping her hand around the thick shaft that she couldn't take in, she sucked hard on his until he groaned.

"Swirl your tongue around me." She did as he instructed. "That's it, baby. Now cup my balls in your hand gently."

They were hot and full, and the more she touched them, the tighter they got to his body. Samuel rocked harder into her mouth, touching the back of her throat every time now. When he held her head to him, his fingers pulling at her hair, she reached between her thighs and touched herself. He cried out when she moaned.

"Come for me, Kennedy. Come so I can feel your release when you scream." She pinched her clit and slid her fingers into her sheath. "That's it, baby, fuck my pretty pussy. Christ, I'm coming."

When he pulled back, she held him to her. She wanted to taste him, feel him come down her throat. As soon as the first hot stream of cum splashed against her tongue, she felt her own climax race over her. Samuel held her tighter the harder he fucked her mouth until her eyes crossed.

As soon as he pulled out of her mouth, he jerked her up and tossed her over the bed on her belly. He was slamming into her pussy from behind almost before she could open for him. His fingers gripped her hips so tight she knew he was going to bruise her, but right now she didn't care. His mouth grazed over her shoulder, and she knew he was going to bite her. When he did, tearing into her flesh hard, she cried out his name and came again. Samuel stiffened behind her and yanked her head up as he marked her again. This time she knew that it would be a mark for all to see. When he came, he lifted his head from her and roared again, the sound of it reverberating around the room several times. His weight dropped on her, and she welcomed it. She was his now and forever.

His laughter had her turned to stare at him. After a quick kiss on the mouth, he rolled to his back. They stared at each other for several seconds before he laughed again.

"We have to go down now." She nodded. "They're not going to be happy with us for making them wait. Not that I care, but you should know that it might make them short with us."

"I don't care. I've just had the most incredible sex in the world, and if they try and fuck this up for me, I'll hurt them all." She watched him stand up and pull clothes on. "I want a shower."

Taking off his clothes that he just pulled on, she smiled at him. "You don't think I'm going down without you do you? I'm taking a shower with you. But no fooling around. They really do need to speak to us."

The shower was quick. She'd tried her best to make him take her again, but he was determined. When she was dried off and dressing, he came up behind her and wrapped his arms around her waist. He held her for several minutes before he spoke.

"The others, the Savages and Jimmy and Kaleb, have asked to be a part of our pride." She turned to look at him. "There are others too, a few, but other species that wish to join us. They need a leader, and they want me to be it."

"But they're not lions, right?" He nodded. "Then I don't understand. How can you be a leader of a group of shifters?"

"We would be the leader, and it can work because both of us have the ability to talk to them. And you, my dear, can talk to all animals." He frowned. "Don't say anything to the council about it. I'm not sure that's anything they need to know."

"Is it a bad thing? That I can do it, I mean. Is it so terrible that I can speak to and listen to all the animals?" He shook his head as he pulled away from her to get his shoes. "Then I doona understand."

When he grinned at her, she knew that she'd slipped again. She had no idea why she bothered trying to hide it from him, but she did. But she did like the way he enjoyed it.

"I don't know, but I have little trust for people that I don't love. I don't know that they will use you somehow, but I don't want to take the chance."

They moved down the stairs, and Butler met them at the bottom. He looked stressed. She felt bad for putting him in this situation. But she realized suddenly that the people in the other room were doing it to him and the rest of the staff. She moved into the living room with one thing on her mind…these people were not going to hurt her people.

The first woman stood up, and Kennedy had the urge to hit her. She had no idea where the need came from, but she pulled it back as far as she could. The second person stood, this one a man, and she watched him pull a notepad from his pocket and look at his watch. Then he wrote in the book. Her temper, not a long one anyway, snapped.

"Cad é an ifreann a cheapann tú go bhfuil tú ag déanamh anseo? Tá mé aon ghá cacamas seo nuair a tá mo maité a gortaíodh agus mé caillte mo dheartháir." Samuel put his hands on her shoulders and whispered *"English, love."* Flushing, she repeated herself. "What the hell do you think you're doing here? I've no need for this crap when my mate has been injured and I've lost me brother."

"We were to understand that you never got along with him. It would seem to us it wouldn't be much of a loss." Her fist came out before she had a moment to think about what she was doing. The man flipped back over the chair he was standing next to and landed in a heap behind the broken thing.

No one moved…not the other members nor Samuel. When someone started to clap their hands, she turned to look at the man she'd not noticed until then. He stood up and walked slowly toward her.

"Kennedy Payne, I presume?" She nodded. "I'm Stephen Silva. I'm happy to finally meet you."

"I doona think I'm going to like you." He laughed and nodded. "What do you want here? There was no reason for him to…I dinna mean…well I did mean to hurt him, but I dinna like what he said."

"Neither did I." The man disappeared and so did the woman. "There, is that better? Shall we start over?"

"What are you doing in our house?" Samuel crossed his arms over his chest as he asked and didn't sit, so neither did she. Stephen did, however, and just as he settled, he let a little of his cat go. Kennedy felt hers tug at her as well.

"You're much stronger than we thought you'd be. Much stronger. Did you know that we've been watching you since we figured out you were Samuel's mate? You've come a long way from the little lost Irish woman to what you are today." Stephen asked them to sit again. "Please. It would go so much better if the two of you would stop trying to figure out whether I'm here to kill you or not."

"Are ye?" He shook his head at her question. "And we're to believe you why? You've given us nothing to know that for sure."

"I haven't, have I?" She sat down, suddenly feeling weak. When Samuel came to her, she waved him off and looked at the man.

"What did you just do to me?" He smiled. "I'm gonna kill you. You undo what you just did to me."

"I cannot. And even if I could, I wouldn't." He stood up then and touched her head. "You're going to be very helpful to the council from now on, Lady Payne. Congratulations to you both."

As he walked to the door, she felt herself grow weaker until she couldn't hold her head up. She heard Samuel yelling her name as she slipped away.

Chapter 16

"He knows." Samuel moved to the side of the bed when Kennedy finally woke up. "He knows everything I can do and what you can do."

"Why? What did he do to you?" She shook her head and then put her hands to it. She looked ill. He held her until she told him she was okay.

"I think he gave me something. I'm not sure, but I think...." She looked at the door, and when it opened his mom moved into the room. She smiled at them both and asked to speak to them.

"Stephen Silva just called here. He said that the council wants to have a meeting with the two of you. He said that he'd like to meet you both." Samuel looked at Kennedy, who shook her head. "He also asked that the two of you have a list of the potential family that wants to join your pride. You've decided to do it then?"

"Yes. I think...we're going to give it a try. When did he say they'd be here?" Samuel's mind was a whirl of questions. He knew that they had to give notice when they came to a home, and he also knew that no one but he and Kennedy would know about the first visit.

"He said they'd be here around dinner time. He said he'd heard that Kennedy was a great cook and wants to know if she could make them something. It's an informal dinner, I guess." His mom started out of the room before turning back. "How are you feeling, sweetheart? Your headache gone?"

"Yes." Kennedy nodded at her, and his mom left the room. As soon as the door shut, Kennedy got up and started to pace the room. He knew she had questions. Hell, so did he, but where to start with them was the kicker.

"I don't have an answer, do you?" She shook her head and laughed. "I doubt this is supposed to be funny. What was you going to say about him giving you something?"

"I can hear them. All of the people in the house, the others in the yard. There are nine bears just outside the perimeter and two wolves. They want to join us. Kaleb is there with them trying to explain that we're lions and that we aren't going to be able to help them. I've let him know to let them come in." She sat down. "I can hear the birds too, as well as the deer and other creatures on the property. They're afraid of the newcomers but think you'll keep them safe."

"Your ability had been enhanced." She nodded at him. "And you think he did it by touching you."

"I think he might have given me a boost, aye. I doona think he wants us to mention that he was here before. I doona know why, but whatever he did, he did on his own." Samuel nodded, thinking she was right. "What do you suppose he's done it for?"

"I don't know, love. And unless he tells us, we might not ever know." He reached for her, and she sat in his lap. "I'm not sure why, but I don't feel as afraid as I did before. Like whatever comes our way we can beat it because we're together."

"I think you might be right." She stood up and smiled at him. "What do I make for a bunch of unwelcome guests for dinner?"

His mom helped with the menu. Butler and Brigitte helped with a grocery list, and before long, there was a large van pulling up by the kitchen door. By three o'clock the kitchen smelled like heaven, and Kennedy was putting together a beautiful cake to go with dinner. Samuel watched her squeeze icing out to form tiny flowers.

"The bears that were here, have you spoken to them yet?" She didn't look up from what she was doing as she asked. "And the wolves are going to move their camper to the Savage campground. Tuck said that he had nineteen campers there now as well as he's rented out three of the cabins."

"I talked to them as well. And so you know, Tuck and Amy have decided that they're going to sell us the campground for just shifters. They seemed to think they'll have more fun than they did with humans." He swiped a flower that she'd yet to put on the cake and moaned as the flavor burst on his tongue. "I may not share that when they get here."

"Are they going to let us run this pride the way we want or are they going to try and take it from us?" Samuel liked that she felt she was a part of this now. He nodded at her question and put out his finger when she'd told him to. After a quick kiss on the tip that had his cock leap to attention, she squirted a long line of the icing she was using. "Are you going to answer me?"

"I will when some blood from my cock goes back to flowing to the rest of my body." She giggled, and he watched her. He'd never heard her do that before. Samuel tried to think what she'd asked him. Then he smiled. "Yes, he'll let us run it the way we want. I'm not sure why I know that but I do."

"I have an idea about something." She bent over to peer in the oven. He could think of about a million ideas on his own. When she turned and caught him staring, she glared. "You have anything on your mind but sex?"

"Nope." She giggled again. "But what did you have on your mind? I'm assuming it's a little less sexual than mine."

"Always. I was thinking that he did this to me because he needed me for this meeting. I think he wants me to know what the others that are coming with him are thinking." Samuel felt his heart skip a couple of beats.

"You think he's bringing danger to our home?" Kennedy shrugged and went back to the cake. "Why do you suppose? I mean if there's a problem with the group, you'd think they could take care of it."

"I doona know if that's what it is, but he's acting like he's never been here before. I'm thinking it has something to do with that." She put down the pastry bag and put the cake under the glass dome. When she started pulling carrots and potatoes out of the refrigerator, he picked up one of the peelers and started peeling the carrots. When she took that job from him and handed him a potato, she started chopping up an onion. He had no idea what they were having for dinner other than beef, but there were enough vegetables for a large crowd. He asked her about it.

"You're not the only species that's going to be at the table. There are a couple of shifters that are not carnivorous." She handed him a carrot and told him to eat it. He put it on the table. "You should eat more vegetables. If we have children, I'm going to make them eat them. So you should get used to it—" He stood up suddenly and grabbed her. "Samuel?"

"You want to have children with me?" She nodded and slapped his shoulder. "When? How soon?"

"When do you want to have them?" He growled low and nipped at her throat. "That soon, huh? After our guests leave, we'll talk about it."

"No, we'll make a baby. Tonight. We'll start on one tonight." He didn't think she was going to agree, but when she nodded, he took her mouth. Christ, he was never going to get enough of this woman. When someone cleared their throat behind him, he turned but didn't let go of Kennedy.

"My Lord, there is a matter of...you should come to the living room, My Lord. Mr. Jimmy and Mr. Kaleb are at it again." Butler looked like he'd gone a round with a tornado. "I believe there is going to be trouble brewing until this is settled."

Kennedy followed him to the living room. It was a mess. Pillows were thrown here and there. A picture frame lay in pieces all over the carpet. And Jimmy and Kaleb were an inch from one another screaming at each other about something. A shrill whistle made the entire room still.

"Now, we're adults here, at least some of us are, and we'll talk like them." When Jimmy started to cut Kennedy off, she raised a brow at him, and he sat down. "I will expect this room to be perfect before our guests get here, and if dinner is burned, I will have the two of you washing dishes and eating only salad for a month. Understand?"

They both nodded at her and lowered their heads. Samuel had to take several deep breaths before he could begin to speak, because this was by far the funniest thing he'd ever seen. When she glared at him, he cleared his throat.

"What's the problem?" Both men started to speak at once, but Kennedy cleared her throat, and they shut up. "Jimmy?"

"He said he was going to be your enforcer. I told him that he couldn't do that, because I was going to do it." Kennedy snorted but Jimmy ignored her. "I've been covering your ass since we met, about five years before he came into the picture."

Kaleb had been watching him as well, so Samuel couldn't understand what the issue was now. When Kennedy stood up and started pacing, Samuel wondered if she knew the heart of this. And when she spoke he knew she did.

"What of me?" Both men looked at him, then back at her. "What do I do for protection? I was hoping that…well, I guess if you want to be Samuel's enforcer, I'll have to find me someone else to watch over me and the *leanai*."

"*Leanai?*" Both men looked at him again while he tried to figure out what it meant. When she snapped the word *children* at them, both men flushed. Samuel watched the two of them as they looked pointedly at her belly.

"You think we can protect ourselves?" Jimmy stood up and was knocked back by Kaleb. "Ye want the job, Kaleb? You'd not watch over Samuel to keep me and the babies safe?"

"It would be an honor, My Lady." He bowed before her and started picking up glass. Jimmy sat there for several seconds before he, too, got up and started picking up the pillows and stuffing that had been spread all over the couch. By the time he and Kennedy went back to the kitchen, he was hurting he was laughing so hard.

"You played them well." She didn't even acknowledge him. "You read their thoughts and knew what the problem was, didn't you?"

"Nay, I did no such thing. You don't think your babies need protecting? I'm shocked at ye you brute of a man. What will I tell the wee ones when they ask me about it?"

"You'll tell them that you're a wicked woman and that you made a grown bear do just what you wanted him to do by fluttering your pretty lashes at him." He kissed her hard, bringing her against his body. "I love you very much, Mrs. Payne."

"And I you, Mr. Payne. Now leave me to my work. We've guests to poison tonight." She was laughing when he left the room. Samuel hoped she was kidding but with her it was hard to tell.

~~~

Kennedy knew the moment that the woman crossed their threshold that she was there to kill Stephen and to blame it on them. When she looked at the man, he winked at her and handed her his coat.

"What a lovely home you have here." She nodded at Lucille Benton as she, too, handed her the cape she'd worn. "I will have to have a tour later. What do you think, Alex? Would you enjoy a tour?"

"Of course, and it's Stephen. As I've told you several hundred times." Lucille laughed a sort of twitter that made Kennedy want to hit her. "I'm sure that the Payne's would love to show us around."

Kennedy started to reach out to the man, but he shook his head. Moving to hand the coats to Butler, she looked at him. He looked worried. There was something else going on, and she was afraid for them all.

What is it? He looked startled for a second, but she continued to talk to him with her mind. *You knew I could do this to others, why not you as well?*

Of course. My Lady, there are four men in the kitchen that look like they mean to take out the house. They claim to be there on behalf of the council, but why would they need such armed guards? He looked back over his shoulder, then at her again. *I don't think this is going to end well.*

It will. Trust me. Kennedy asked to be excused by her guest and moved to the door to the kitchen. The men had come with Lucille. Moving into the kitchen, she looked at them, then at the mess they'd made in her kitchen. "You will clean that up."

The man in front only snorted at her and told her to go to hell. Before she could answer him, she felt someone touch her mind, but rather than speak, they sent her a mental picture. Reaching out to the first man, she touched his head and he dropped like a stone. The other three were easy enough to do the same thing to, and in a matter of seconds, they were being tied up by the kitchen help.

She was just making her way to the living room again with Butler carrying a tray of appetizers when another picture entered her mind. This one was a heart, and she smiled. Someone wanted to thank her.

"There you are. We were beginning to worry about you." Kennedy looked at Lucille as she sat nearly atop of Stephen. "Weren't we, dear?"

"I'm not your dear, and I wasn't concerned. This is her home." Stephen stood up and walked to the fireplace. "I understand you've only just lost your brother, Mrs. Payne. I am sorry for your loss. It must be hard to lose one so close to you."

"Aye, and I thank you. We were never close, he and I, but he was blood. And you have heard about the Irish and their blood. Stronger than their ale." Stephen laughed, and Lucille only looked confused.

"You're not distraught over his death? I would have thought that you'd be out of your mind with sorrow." Kennedy shook her head and felt the woman's anger surge forward. "I'd be crazy with his loss. If I had a brother, that is."

"Oh but you do, don't you?" Lucille looked at her, then at the room. "Ye've a brother. Two, I think. At least that's what I was to understand from the older one."

Kennedy knew that she had a knife on her. She'd felt the danger of it when she'd walked in the room just now. And when she stood up and moved toward Stephen, she knew that she and Samuel were right, she was there to kill him.

"I've no idea what you're talking about." Butler came into the room just then and announced dinner. Samuel came toward her to escort her in, but she reached for Stephen. He smiled at her and shook his head.

"You're a vixen, has anyone told you that before?" Kennedy didn't answer him right away, explaining to Samuel what was going on. He told her she was going to pay for this, and she felt his arousal through their connection.

"Aye, they have, but I only improve over time." She sat when he pulled out her chair and was happy to see that she'd pissed off Lucille more. When the salads were cleared away and dinner was served, Kennedy decided to spice things up a bit.

"I thought there would be more of you here tonight. You don't travel with armed guard?" She handed the bowl of carrots to Lucille as she asked. The woman nearly dropped the bowl on the table. Kennedy smiled at her. "At least someone to watch over you as you visit other people's homes."

"We do sometimes, but with the two of you, we felt it wouldn't be all right." Stephen declined the carrots but did take the potatoes. "I understand you and Samuel are headed to Ireland soon."

"Aye, in a week. We're going for our honeymoon. Samuel's never seen the manor." Stephen nodded and cut into his beef and moaned. Lucille started to stand up, but Kennedy put her hand on her arm. "I wouldn't if I were you."

The woman stared at her, as did the rest of the people around the table. Lucille tried to pull away, but Kennedy reached down and took the knife from her. Picking it up by the handle, she tossed it to the wall and watched as it quivered there for a few seconds.

"You think you know something?" Lucille laughed. "You know nothing. Donny. Andy. Come in now."

Everyone stared at the door that Lucille had been shouting at. The kitchen door moved and she smiled, but when Brigitte walked through with a pitcher of tea in her hands, Lucille tried to pull free again.

"They're tied up." She looked at her, then at the door again as Kennedy continued. "I had them tied up and their weapons taken from them. Also, the knives in your coat have been removed."

"No. You couldn't have. They were our best men." Kennedy didn't let go of Lucille but held her while she nodded to Samuel. He got up from the table and went to the kitchen. When he returned, he was carrying a chair with a man strapped to it, and yanked the tape off his mouth.

"She knew we was here. Came right in and put us out." The man in the chair looked at Stephen. "She made us do this. Said if we didn't, we'd have to pay with our lives and that of our families."

"He lies." Kennedy looked at Stephen at Lucille's outburst. "I don't know what he's talking about. Come on, Stephen, we should leave."

"Kennedy?" Stephen watched her. Kennedy looked at Samuel before she looked at Stephen again. This was going to be an all-out war, she just knew it.

"They're in it together. She plans to kill you and make it look like Samuel and I did it. If we're found guilty of these crimes, we'll have to turn over everything to the council and we'll have nothing. Which would be all right, I suppose, since she plans to have us put to death." She looked at Samuel as she continued. "Lucille isn't a true shifter. She's a turned lion. Your father hurt her, and the only way to get back at him since I killed him was to hurt you."

Stephen snapped his fingers and three guards were suddenly in the room. As Lucille was being taken away, he sat calmly in the chair and then ordered the other men to be taken too. After they were all gone, he asked to have more beef. Butler nearly leapt at the chance to serve the man.

Chapter 17

Stephen watched the couple as they tried for things to be normal. He was so relieved that it was over that he found he had an appetite again, the first he'd had in nearly three months. When dessert was served and he'd gorged himself on three slices of the best cake he'd ever eaten, he leaned back in his chair.

"I'm sorry." Kennedy looked ready to burst with anger, but it was Samuel that exploded on him.

"You motherfucker, you should be sorry. What the fuck was that all about? You must have known what she was up to, yet you bring her here to what, have someone, one of my family, get hurt?" Samuel stood up, and Kennedy stepped in front of him.

"He didn't do it for that." She turned to him. "Did ye? You were testing us. You were looking to see if we were loyal to the pride."

"I was. But there's more. I would like you both to be a part of the council. Not on it, per se, but a part of the group that governs us." Samuel sat down, and Kennedy said no. "You should think about it. I can give you whatever you wish in standards of—"

"I have all I want right here." Samuel pulled Kennedy to his lap. "And that being said, I think I'd like for you to leave and never come back."

"I'll give you free run of the pride. All of it. You'll never pay dues, never answer to us for minor things, and you'll lead a group of your choosing." He hoped that they'd do it for that reason and held onto his last thing to bribe them with.

"Nay. He said no, and we'd like you to leave now." Stephen stood up and laid the last bit in front of them. Samuel picked it up and then laid it back down.

"You'd do that?" Stephen nodded and sat back down. "For how long?"

"Until you've no more descendants." Kennedy picked the document up, read it over, and looked at them both. "I'll even include any step-children you might have in the mix."

Stephen wasn't sure that he had them. He wanted them, and he'd do most anything to have them work for him, including giving them something that he knew neither of them would guess he'd already given them.

"We'll need to talk this over." He nodded at Samuel and stood up. Butler came out of the kitchen with a container, and when he looked inside, he nearly moaned. "Kennedy thought you'd like a bit for your lunch tomorrow."

"Thank you." He was moving out to his car when Samuel said his name. When he turned, he watched the man struggle with whatever he wanted to ask.

"Did you plan this? Did you know that she was going to try and have you killed?" He shook his head. "Then why did you do that to Kennedy?"

"I didn't do anything to her about her ability, an ability that you have had all along." Samuel shook his head, and Stephen laughed. "You never looked beyond what you thought you could do. Kennedy simply tried and found out what I've known all your life."

"Then what did you do to her?" The limo driver opened the door for him, but he stood there thinking about whether or not to answer Samuel's question. Then he smiled.

"I'll tell you when you give me your answer. Yes or no, I'll give you the answer when you do to me." He slipped into the car before Samuel could hurt him. This was deliciously fun.

"Will they do it?" Stephen watched the woman materialize in the seat across from him and smiled at her question. "Do you think they'll do what we want?"

"I do. I'm not sure they'll be as easy as you think they will, but they will agree." She nodded and smiled. "You're pleased?"

"I am. I've wanted this for them for a very long time." Stephen nodded. "And the baby, did you tell them about the baby?"

"No. But I will when he calls me. They're both going to be very surprised when they find out." He laughed hardily. "I think he may kill me anyway."

"I think they'll be very happy no matter what." She shimmered out of the limo only to reappear seconds later. "I think I should like to meet them soon. Maybe when you tell them about the children."

"I can arrange that for you, My Lady." She nodded and disappeared. Yes, Stephen thought, this was going to be a great deal of fun.

～～～

"What do you think?" Samuel had read over the papers that appeared on the table after Stephen left three times and couldn't find a thing wrong with them. He looked up at Kennedy when she asked him again.

"We get paid for being there when they need us. We don't have to go anywhere other than the council house when there are meetings and report back to them after it's over. No one will know about us but him and another person. I don't know." He tossed the papers on the table. "It all seems too one sided and in our favor."

"I doona like it." He knew that, she'd told him that several times, and he had to agree with her. He dinna like it either. Then he laughed at what he'd thought. He was beginning to sound like her.

"They're paying the upkeep on the manor and this house forever so long as we continue to have children and they have children. There will be care given to our offspring while we're called to the meetings, and a car will be provided for us wherever we go." He picked the papers up again to see if he'd missed anything. "Oh, and apparently our abilities will be passed down to our oldest child, boy or girl, and their oldest will be given the same."

She sat down and stood up again. He knew she was going to ask him what he'd done to her, but he didn't have an answer for that either. As soon as they made a decision, they'd find out.

"I think we should do it." He nodded at her when she finally spoke. "We have little risk and much to gain."

"We do. And I don't know why, but that scares me a little." She told him it scared her a great deal. "Well, do we call him?"

"Aye, do it." He reached for his cell phone and realized he had no idea how to contact the man. Calling for Butler, he asked him and said he'd not left a number for him when he'd called either. Samuel was about to go to his office when Stephen suddenly appeared in the room.

"Christ, don't do that again." He bowed before them, and Samuel asked him to have a seat. "We've decided to—"

"There is someone that wishes to meet you." Samuel looked at Kennedy, then back at Stephen. "You'll be working for her too. In fact, she's the one that thought of the two of you."

Samuel nodded when Kennedy did. The man had only left an hour ago, but he looked like he'd been ready for bed. His jammies suddenly disappeared and he was in a suit again. He apologized and nodded.

The woman that shimmered into the room commanded respect. Not that she'd said a word but she simply looked like it. Samuel found himself bowing before her.

"Get up, young man. You too, Lady Kennedy. Look at the two of you all grown up." She smiled, and Samuel felt it all the way to his toes. "I'm ever so glad that you've decided to help me. I had hoped that you would."

"You're very welcome," Kennedy said and looked at Samuel before she continued. "And who do ye be?"

"Oh my, that would help, wouldn't it?" the woman said. "I'm ever so sorry. I'm Mother Nature." Samuel looked at Stephen, then at the woman again. "But you can call me Clare."

About the Author

Kathi Barton, author of the bestselling series Force of Nature, lives in Nashport, Ohio with her husband Paul. In addition to writing full time Kathi likes to spend time with her eight grandkids, three children and three children-in-laws. She writes to relax and have fun.

Her muse, a cross between Jimmy Stewart and Hugh Jackman brings them to life for her readers in a way that has them coming back time and again for more. Her favorite genre is paranormal romance with a great deal of spice. You can visit Kathi on line and drop her an email if you'd like. She loves hearing from her fans. aaronskiss@gmail.com.

Follow Kathi on her blog:
http://kathisbartonauthor.blogspot.com/